Praise for
Confessions of a Cereal Mother

"A realistic and humorous take on motherhood. Are you in my house?!?"

—Robin O'Bryant, author of indie best-seller
Ketchup is a Vegetable and Other Lies Moms Tell Themselves

"Delightfully humorous with truths about motherhood and womanhood. You'll immediately be hooked with her fun storytelling and hilarious hooks. A truly fantastic read that will not only lift your motherly spirit, but also remind you what motherhood is truly all about . . . and it's all worth it."

—Karie Elordi, author of the popular blog
"The Dating Divas" www.thedatingdivas.com

Other books by Rachel McClellan:

Fractured Light

Fractured Soul

Fractured Truth
(coming 2014)

Confessions of a

CEREAL MOTHER

Confessions of a

CEREAL MOTHER

Rachel McClellan

PLAIN SIGHT PUBLISHING
An Imprint of Cedar Fort, Inc.
Springville, Utah

ISBN 13: 978-1-4621-1115-2

Published by Plain Sight Publishing, an imprint of Cedar Fort, Inc.
2373 W. 700 S., Springville, UT 84663
Distributed by Cedar Fort, Inc., www.cedarfort.com

LIBRARY OF CONGRESS CATALOGING-IN-PUBLICATION DATA

McClellan, Rachel, 1977- author.
[Short stories. Selections]
Confessions of a cereal mother / Rachel McClellan.
   pages cm
ISBN 978-1-4621-1115-2
1. Motherhood--Fiction. I. Title.

PS3613.C3582C66 2013
813'.6--dc23

2012048260

Cover design by Erica Dixon
Cover design © 2013 Lyle Mortimer
Edited by Emily S. Chambers
Typeset by Breanna Trost

Printed in the United States of America

10 9 8 7 6 5 4 3 2 1

Printed on acid-free paper

To my husband, who keeps me around
with weekly eggnog and toast.

Contents

Introduction

My name is Mommy. I used to be called by another, but my former name disappeared the moment I held my firstborn child. If you are a mother, then you understand. If not, then I will attempt to explain why I was willing to give up my given name for the unknown infant lying in my arms.

It wasn't because my baby was cute. In fact, my firstborn was rather ugly. He had slits for eyes, a Planet-of-the-apes monkey nose, and a head that looked like a Barbie's when you squish it between your fingers. But when my husband handed me our odd-looking baby boy and I wrapped my arms around his small helpless body, I *knew*. I knew I would give up all that I had, including my life, to protect this child, and every other child God blessed me with.

I'm not a perfect mother. Far from it. My girls don't have perfectly styled hair, and my boys often wear their jeans three days in a row (I do make them change their underwear—most of the time). On busy nights, my kids eat cold cereal for dinner, and sometimes, for breakfast, they eat the brownies I made at midnight the night before when I finally had an hour to myself to watch *The Biggest Loser*. But I do my best.

Mommy is a loaded word. Just thinking the word makes me smile, cry, laugh, and scream. There are so many emotions wrapped up into those five letters that sometimes I think I might go mad, but no matter how many times I hear that word, no matter the circumstance, I would never trade it for any other.

This is my life.

I am Mommy.

1

You Can Never Go Back

It all began with a dimple, and not just any dimple. One so big and deep, you'd hardly notice the smile next to it. I didn't know that falling in love with that seemingly endless hole in my future husband's cheek would be the cause of all my life's grief and happiness. On any given day I'm either cursing that dimple or kissing it.

Today I want to kiss it.

"We have to have sex right now," I say to my husband when I find him in the garage. We've been trying to get pregnant for months but have found the task to be rigorous and methodical—like being on our honeymoon with a drill sergeant.

"But I'm working on the car."

"Same skill set." I remove the screwdriver in his hand. "It's the sixth of the month, I just had a twinge of pain in my right ovary, and my temperature is up a tenth of a degree. It's now or never."

It takes a couple of months, but finally I am late. By ten minutes. So I quickly do my business on my dollar store pregnancy test and wait for those double touchdown lines to appear.

Still waiting.

Two minutes feel like hours, and I've read the direction so many times that I wonder if the French version might make more sense. When nothing appears in the magic white window, I think I've wasted another dollar. Angry and disgusted, I toss it into the garbage.

If only there had been a camera installed in our bathroom (there wouldn't have been—we're not that type), I might've seen my husband visit the toilet shortly after me. While there, he finds the pregnancy test, and without reading any stupid instructions discovers that I'm pregnant. Because he thinks I'm planning some sort of surprise, he says nothing to me until a week later when he can't stand it anymore.

"So, when were you going to tell me?" he says during the halftime show of a playoff game.

I stuff a cheese puff into my mouth. "Tell you what?" I look down into an empty bag. Not the single serving kind either, the family econo size. "Did I really just eat the whole bag?"

He takes it from me and crumbles it up. "That doesn't surprise me, considering, but you should watch what you eat."

"What's that supposed to mean?"

He turns the volume down on the television. "I know you're probably planning some big surprise, but the longer you go without telling me, the more I think it's not mine."

"What's not yours?"

"The baby."

"What baby?"

"Are you seriously going to pretend like you don't know what I'm talking about?"

"I really have no idea what you're talking about."

He scans my face. "You really don't know?"

I frown and shake my head. "What?"

He turns away, hunched over and rubbing his hands. "This is too good. I think I'll keep it a secret. See how long it takes you to figure it out."

"Figure what out?"

"Nothing." He walks to the kitchen.

I follow. "You better tell me."

He opens the fridge. "No way."

"Tell me or we're having a wrestling match right now."

He removes mayo and a package of bologna. "No can do."

I take the bologna from him and open it up. "No you can't tell me, or no you won't wrestle me?"

"Both."

"Since when did you chicken out from a fight?" I roll up a bologna disk and take a bite. Actually, I eat the whole thing.

"I don't fight 'frail people,' Aaron says, eyeing me. "Make sure you chew before you swallow."

I swallow. "Frail?"

"How long ago was your period?"

I shrug. "I don't know. I thought it should've been a week ago, but I must've kept track wrong."

He smiles really big and gives me a hug. "You're pregnant!"

I push him away. "Get out! There's no way."

"Yes, you are."

"How in the world would you know?"

"I found your pregnancy test."

"But it didn't show anything!"

"How long did you wait?"

"Forever."

"Forever is not that long for you."

I pause, trying not to smile. "So, I'm pregnant?"

He grins and nods.

"We're having a baby?"

He laughs. "Yup!"

I throw my arms around him, unable to contain my glee.

The next several months drag on more than any other time in my life. I spend most of my time on the Internet, visiting every pregnancy forum I can find. I'm convinced every ache or pain is because there's something wrong with my baby. Even my ingrown toenail.

When anyone asks me how far along I am, I answer precisely: seven months, two weeks, three days, forty-nine minutes, and six seconds. But I don't stop there. I proceed to give them a detailed account of how I'm feeling, the constant sickness, the hunger, the frequent visits to the bathroom, and—of course—the weight gain.

Because it's my first baby, I eat everything in sight, believing the same lie every other first-time pregnant woman has heard. "You're eating for two," an elderly woman tells me. I thank her for the seemingly great advice and eat everything in my path, much like a lawn mower cuts grass. And when I gain seventy pounds and it takes me years to loose it, I make sure to share the same advice with any pregnant women I encounter.

When thirty-four weeks comes, I think every stomach cramp is labor. I've already been to the hospital twice, only to be sent home. At thirty-six weeks, or nine months, I worry when I haven't gone into labor.

"Do you think I'll have to have a C-section?" I ask my older sister over the telephone.

"Why?"

"Because I'm already nine months pregnant and don't feel close to having the baby!"

She laughs.

"What's so funny?"

She calms down. "Full-term is forty weeks."

"Wait." I grab my belly. "What?"

"Technically it's *ten* months. Haven't you been listening to your doctor?"

"He talks too much. And since when is it ten months? I've always heard nine."

"They say that so women will get pregnant. Sort of like the $9.99 bargain deal. It sounds much better than $10."

"So, I have to be miserable and fat for four more weeks?"

"Welcome to motherhood."

But I don't have to wait forty weeks, only thirty-nine. My doctor is going on vacation and he's explained to me that he can either induce me or let the on-call doctor, whom I've never met, deliver my baby. Because I'm afraid to have someone I don't know deliver my baby, I choose to be induced—a decision I later regret.

Aaron and I arrive at the hospital on a Friday morning. While my husband completes a barrage of paperwork, I'm being "prepped," much like a turkey on Thanksgiving Day. After I dress in the least flattering gown in the world, they give me an IV of Pitocin to get my contractions started. And start they do. I feel real labor now, and it makes me feel foolish for going into the hospital before. The pain I felt before was frosting compared to the pound cake hammering me now.

"Do you want an epidural?" a nurse asks.

I've gone back and forth on this decision for some time, but as I stare down at my global-size belly, I have a funny feeling that the monster inside me (I'm hurting right now, so forgive me for not saying "sweet child") isn't going to come out willingly. I don't hesitate. "Yes, please, and tell the drug guy I'll name my kid after him if he gets here fast."

When the nurse anesthetist arrives and asks me to roll into a tight ball, I laugh. "Have you seen me?"

From behind his back he shows me a six-inch-long needle. "Have you seen this?"

I cower. "What is that?"

"This is what I put into your spine to make the pain go away. And the tighter the ball, the easier it is for me to hit the right spot and not paralyze you for life." He smiles.

I roll up into a tight ball, my legs practically behind my head.

"Don't worry," he says. "You'll feel better in about five minutes."

Thankfully, he's right. Just to be sure, I tell Aaron to give me a few hard slaps on my legs. "Come on, it will be funny," I say.

"Did they give you something besides an epidural?" He wiggles a few of my toes.

"I'm just bored. How long do you think this will take?"

"You're having a baby, not getting an oil change. Relax."

I do as he says, enduring the time by reading and watching TV, but hours pass with little progress. The only exciting thing to happen are two nurses who come in to "check" me every hour, but the last few times they've brought company. "We have student nurses with us today. Do you mind if they check you too?" the nurse asks.

I look into the eyes of all the eager young nurses, their fingers wiggling in anticipation. I shrug. "Have at it. Someone might as well feel like they've accomplished something today."

Eleven hours pass and I'm only dilated to a seven. Thinking that's normal, I don't worry.

Until my doctor comes to visit.

He says hello but frowns when he discovers how little I've progressed. He turns to the nurse. "Why isn't she further along?"

The nurse shrugs. "I guess she's not ready."

His lips press together. "Let's get this done. Increase the Pitocin." He turns to me. "I need you to push when I say, okay? I'm going to break your water now."

I swallow but can't help but giggle when a gush of water flows from the table onto the floor. "That's funny."

"Sorry, my wife acts weird during stressful situations," my husband says.

The doctor's all business and doesn't acknowledge Aaron or me. I also notice his brow is now as tight as his lips. My heart begins to pound.

"I want you to push hard for ten seconds. Are you ready?"

I manage a nod.

"Now!"

I push really hard and then gasp for breath after ten seconds. But I don't have time to rest.

"Push again," the doctor says, his eyes darting back and forth between the baby's heart monitor and my stomach. "Now!"

I push again as hard as I can. We do this several times

until the doctor finally stops me. He turns to the nurse. "Has the baby's heartbeat been dropping like this all day?"

"Dropping?" I say, but no one hears me.

The nurse shifts her weight. "Only when we'd increase the Pitocin."

The Doctor's voice rises. "And you didn't tell me?"

The nurse doesn't answer; she's apparently too busy swallowing her nerves.

"Outside, please," he tells the nurse and then turns to me. "Everything's going to be okay, but we need to get the baby out ASAP. You're having a C-section."

Before I can respond, he leaves the room, closing the door behind him, but in his hurry it doesn't close all the way. We hear him speaking from inside our room.

"What is wrong with you?" the doctor yells. "Something is clearly wrong with the baby!" He slams something hard against the counter of the nurse's station. I imagine the nurses jumping as much as I do.

Aaron takes my hand.

"Get the OR and have them prep a room right away!" the doctor says.

When the nurse returns, her hands shake as she prepares me for surgery. Her nervousness makes me nervous. "Aaron?" I say.

"You and the baby will be fine. Don't worry," he whispers in my ear.

I want to believe him, but everything is happening so fast. I'm being swarmed by all sorts of medical staff, and within two minutes I'm in an operating room—without my husband.

"Where's Aaron?" I ask, hoping someone's listening.

"He'll be here in a minute. He's gowning up," a nurse says.

After a minute and still no husband, I begin to panic, especially when they strap my arms down. Everyone's talking at once so I can't ask why that's necessary, but I soon find out why.

Just then a sheet drops below my neck to prevent me from seeing what's about to happen. I hear metal clinking against metal, the shuffling of feet, and then someone grunting. If I wouldn't have been in my current predicament, I would've thought someone was being murdered behind that solid white sheet.

But it wasn't murder; just someone taking a knife to my belly.

I can't feel anything, but suddenly my whole body is being lifted up as the doctor tries to remove—more like tear out—my baby; only the straps keep me in place. This happens several times. The sensation of being lifted and then dropped is so unnatural that I'm even more afraid. Tears roll down the sides of my face, and I'd give anything to have my husband near me.

But then I hear a baby cry.

The doctor peeks around the curtain, hair and eyes as wild as Mr. Oz's. "Congratulations! You have a beautiful baby boy." He motions to someone in the corner. Finally my husband is at my side. Apparently he'd been in the room the whole time but out of my line of sight.

Aaron smooths back my hair and asks the doctor, "What was the problem?"

"The umbilical chord was wrapped around his neck multiple times," the doctor explains. "Every time your wife contracted, the cord would constrict, causing the baby's heartbeat to drop. The cord was also preventing the baby from dropping into the birth canal." He hands Aaron our new baby. "Your son looks healthy, but we'd like to check him out as soon as possible just to be sure."

Aaron nods. "Meet your son, Mommy." He moves the baby to where I can see him, but I can barely make him out through my tears. I blink and my vision clears.

"Is he okay?"

"It looks that way. How are you doing?"

I give him a weak smile.

"Will you be okay if I stay with the baby?"

"Of course."

"I'll come find you as soon as I can."

I nod. My husband leans over and kisses my cheek. "You did good."

I watch him carry my son out of the room until they disappear. It's hard seeing them leave. Months of waiting only to have my child taken away. *It's just for a little while*, I remind myself and take a deep breath.

It takes ten minutes for the doctor to sew me up, and during this time, he tries to make conversation, but all I can think about is my new son. I feel like I've already forgotten what he looks like.

When the doctor finishes, a nurse wheels my bed into a small room not much bigger than a closet. It smells like one too. I look around for a broom and mop.

The nurse seems to sense my anxiety. "This isn't the room you'll be staying in. This is just temporary until your room upstairs is ready."

"Thanks," I say. "Do you know when I'll get to see my baby?"

"Soon. Your husband will bring him in when he can. Do you need anything?"

I'm starting to shake but think that's normal, so I don't say anything. "I'm good."

"Here's your call light if you need anything," she says and then leaves.

As the seconds pass, my shaking increases and the room turns cold. I'm just starting to get feeling back into my lower extremities and discover that the table I'm on is much too short for my legs. My feet are dangling into nothing, and the thin sheet covering me doesn't offer any protection from the cold.

I lift my hand to press the call light, but the motion makes me shake even harder, and my jittery fingers knock the button out of reach. Soon my whole body vibrates like a struck tuning fork. And it's not just my outsides. Every nerve in my body is humming to the point where it hurts.

Because I can't do much else, I focus on a wall clock across from the bed. The second hand becomes my anchor, keeping me from loosing my sanity.

One.

Two.

Three.

I watch each tick, acknowledging only the passing seconds and not my spazzing body that seems to be seizing out of control. And for every second that passes, I experience a small moment of relief; for I know I will never have to experience those same painful sixty seconds again. That's how life is sometimes—enduring minutes.

Twenty rotations go by and I'm still alone, worrying about my baby and shaking worse than a gyrator hand-weight.

Finally a door opens, and in walks my husband holding a tight bundle. Aaron is smiling big: a proud father. "Do you want to hold your son?" he asks.

I sort of nod and try to reach out but can't.

"What's wrong?" he asks.

"I . . . I'm shaking," I stutter, but even speaking makes my insides quiver more.

"Is that normal?" Aaron asks, worried.

My eyes plead.

Aaron picks up the call light from the side of the bed and pages a nurse. When he notices me staring longingly at our baby boy, he lays him next to me where I can see his face. His perfectly skinny, hairless face.

A nurse knocks on the door and comes in. "Can I help you?" she asks.

"My wife is shaking. Is that normal?"

She frowns and performs a quick assessment. "It can be. She's been on a lot of medication for hours, endured labor and a C-section. Her body's probably in shock. It should go away in a couple of hours."

"Cold," I mumble.

"I'll bring in some blankets." She turns to leave but then stops. "Oh, your mom and sisters are in the hall. Would you like to see them?"

I want to, but even thinking about trying to talk to them makes me shake. "Later," I say.

"I'll go talk to them," Aaron says. "I'll be back in a minute."

Out in the hall, I hear Aaron trying to explain why they can't see me.

"You can't keep me from my sister!" my little sister's voice says.

"I'm not trying to keep you from her," Aaron says. "She doesn't feel well enough for visitors."

I can practically see my little sister pressing a finger into his chest. "You better not turn out to be a controlling husband. Nobody messes with my sister!"

"Chill out, Liane," my other sister says. "We'll come back in a couple of hours."

They say their good-byes, and then Aaron returns. "Your sister is psycho," he says.

I try to smile.

Like the nurse said, several hours later I feel better, but more important, I've held my baby. I've caressed his body, counted his fingers and toes, and memorized his face. I've forgotten all about the last ten months of sleepless nights, hunger, and pain. My baby is here, and my life will never be the same.

I am a mommy.

2

I Dream about Sleep

I used to be anal about sleep. "Eight hours! I must have my eight hours!" I'd cry to whomever would listen.

I'd convinced myself that if I didn't have eight hours of sleep, then I wouldn't be able to function for the rest of the day. I even insisted TV be banned from our bedroom, much to my husband's dismay. "I can't sleep with any sounds or lights," I'd complain.

Sheesh, was I spoiled.

Three months ago I had my first child. He sleeps okay, I think. It's not like I've been a mother before. He typically wakes me up a couple of times a night, but for the last week he's needed me multiple times.

Tonight I'm going to try and keep him awake as long as possible, figuring he'll sleep longer, which means I can sleep longer. But his eyes look heavy and his breathing is steady. *Too steady.* It's only nine o'clock, and if he sleeps now, then he'll wake up at midnight, and his whole schedule will be off. As it is, I'm running on only about four hours of sleep a night and that's often interrupted. I desperately need just one solid block.

I unwrap the blanket from around my son and proceed to stretch out his limbs. "Wake up, little one."

His arms and legs snap back into a fetal position, and he closes his eyes.

"Oh no, you don't." I pick him up and bounce him on my knee. His chubby brow furrows and his bottom lip curls out. I continue the motion, stopping only when my leg tires, but the moment I slow, his eyes droop and roll into the back of his head.

"Wake up, wake up," I sing and bounce.

His lip begins to quiver, but I keep bouncing and singing. His fists ball tight and his toes curl inward.

I sing:

"Stay awake little baby, stay awake little baby. You better not sleep or your mama's gonna freak; five hours is all I really need."

His little lungs produce a war-like cry, grating on my already shaken nerves. They vibrate just beneath my skin, and I wonder how much more I can take. I stand and walk him around the living room. This preoccupies him, but after a few minutes I'm too exhausted and have to sit down. He begins to cry again.

Just put him to bed and let him cry, I hear my older sister's voice say in my head.

"But he's only three months!"

So? He'll survive, but you won't. You need to get some rest.

I stand up again, despite my tired bones. What does my sister know anyway? She may have already raised three kids, but none of them are nearly as sweet as mine. I can see how she ignores hers so easily.

"Everything okay?" my husband asks as he walks out of

the bedroom and into the living room. "Do you want me to take him?"

I seriously consider it but think better of it. He worked a night shift the day before and then studied for school all day. I know I'm tired, but so is he. "No. I got it. You've been up all night and day. Why don't you go to bed?"

He rubs my back. "I can help. Really."

"Thanks, but I've got this." I jiggle the baby harder when his cry grows louder.

My husband frowns. "Just let me know." He kisses us both then returns to our room.

I almost burst into tears. *Stay!* I want to yell. I so want his help but can't ask for it. I'm the mom. This is my job. All other moms seem to do just fine, so what's my problem?

After ten more minutes of trying to soothe my fussy baby, I decide to just let him sleep. I change him, wrap him tight, and try to breastfeed him, but he falls asleep.

"Come on, baby. You have to eat." I try to force it, but it's no use.

Defeated, I tuck him in and turn on the baby monitor. I can't wait to go to bed, but my motherly duties are not over. I switch the laundry, wash the dishes, straighten the house; everything must reflect that I'm a perfect mother and wife.

At last my jobs are complete. I quietly open my bedroom door and slip into bed next to my sleeping husband. It's eleven o'clock. I take only three deep breaths before I'm asleep.

Peace.

I wake suddenly, my heart pounding. The fire alarm is going off! I shake my head. No, the baby is crying. I look at the clock. Midnight.

I ignore my frighteningly tight nerves and go to the baby. He's kicked off all his blankets and is fighting the air blindly. I cuddle him to my chest and sit down in a nearby rocking chair. This time he drinks eagerly, gulping and slurping like he's been wandering in the desert for weeks.

"Easy there, kid," I say. "Save some for later." I stroke his soft skin until I doze off. I wake when the baby begins to cough. He too has fallen back asleep and must've choked on milk pooling in his cheek. I'm too tired to burp him, so I return him to bed and float to my own.

I'm asleep instantly. It's 12:30.

At 1:10 my eyes open. Baby is crying again. I pretend I don't hear—for almost sixty seconds, and then I have to get out of bed. My baby needs me.

Once again I pick up my child and try to determine what he needs. His diaper is a little wet so I change him. He still cries. I wrap him tight and try to feed him again, but he's not interested. Rocking isn't helping either. I stand up, teeter slightly, and then walk around the darkened room, patting his back. A moment later he lets out a monstrous burp.

Right. I'd forgotten that important step.

I hold him in front of me. "Feel better?" His big blue eyes stare back at me. I cradle him to my chest and walk around. I'm too tired to sing, but I'm afraid if I don't do something I'll fall asleep while walking. I think of the easiest thing I know how to do—counting: *One, two, three, four . . .* baby is quiet so I tell myself to count to a hundred and then lay him down. *Surely he'll be asleep by then,* I think.

I reach one hundred and gently place him in his crib. His eyes are wide open. I step away from the crib but still within view and hope he'll go to sleep on his own. But it doesn't take long for his brow and lips to tighten again, followed by a heart-breaking cry.

I start the process all over again, starting with number one. *Just get through the next one hundred seconds,* I tell myself. My time limit comes, but I can tell by my son's breathing that he's not quite asleep. I count again.

Finally, his breathing is steady, and I lay him down as carefully as I can. I'm practically holding my breath as I slowly withdraw. It takes me a full five minutes before I'm out of his room, as I'm convinced any floor board creak will wake him.

Exhausted, I make it back to bed. It's 1:50 a.m. "Please, heaven," I say. "Let me get some sleep." A single tear makes it to my pillow just as my eyes close.

It's not even thirty minutes later and baby is awake, crying. I sit up, shaking. My nerves are shot. I look to my sleeping husband and contemplate waking him. But in the end, I choose not to. I can do this.

I feed the baby again, thinking that's what he needs. It takes a full hour to get him asleep. During this time, my mind wanders to a dark place. I don't know how much longer I can do this. My whole body hums with exhaustion, and I'm too tired to even cry. Something's wrong with me. I don't remember other moms complaining about how tired they are. Maybe I wasn't meant to be a mom. I'm clearly not strong enough.

My baby lets out a long sigh, and I know he's asleep. I lay him down and crawl back into bed. I can't sleep, however. I keep thinking I hear the baby crying. It's not long before my imagination becomes a reality.

Baby's awake.

Again.

But I can't move.

I stare into the darkness, begging to be a part of it.

Baby cries louder.

I wish the mattress would swallow me and take me to Alice's wonderland. Tim Burton's version. With Johnny Depp.

Suddenly I'm being elbowed. I remain still.

"The baby's crying," my husband mumbles.

And?

I stay motionless. Dead.

Another nudge. "Wake up. The baby's crying," he says louder.

I'm a log, drifting in the calm waters on a high mountainous lake.

"Honey?"

My husband sits up. He takes hold of my hand, lifts it into the air and then drops it. It flops to the bed. A dead fish.

Suddenly he's shaking me, his voice alert. "Wake up!"

Like Lazarus, my eyes open, and I can't help but laugh.

And then cry.

"What's going on?" my husband asks.

I choke on my tears. "I'm too exhausted. I've been up with the baby multiple times, and I'm going on days without much sleep. I can't do it anymore. I'm so sorry." I bury my face into my pillow.

"Why didn't you say something? I could've helped." He smooths my hair. "Get some rest. I'll take care of the baby." After a quick hug, he leaves.

The words "I failed" lull me to sleep as my eyes close on a cold, wet pillow.

I wake up. The time is 8:30 a.m. I spring from bed, heart racing. I can't hear the baby. Surely he should be awake by now, at least that's what my full breasts are telling me. The pain is so sharp I'm half tempted to perform a mastectomy on myself. But first I have to check on the baby.

I find him lying on my husband's chest. Both of them have fallen asleep on the couch, the television turned low to the sports channel.

I smile and breathe. He's fine. Baby survived without me. The solid five hours of sleep have helped me see things in a better light, and I don't feel so hopeless. Or worthless.

Five hours. That's all I needed. I laugh now when I hear someone complain that they didn't get their eight hours of sleep. *Have a baby*, I want to say, along with a few other choice words.

But I don't.

I survived, and so will they.

3

A Smelly Poltergeist

My eyes snap open. Darkness surrounds me, but I know its morning. I heard the house inhale its first breath of the day: water rushing through the pipes below my bedroom. A child has flushed a toilet.

I'm afraid to look at the clock. Afraid it will reveal a time much too early for a child to be awake. The kind of day I have is determined by how early my children wake up.

I say "children," plural, because I know their routine. One of them wakes. Sees it's still dark outside. Hears that no one else is up.

Especially Mommy.

Free reign.

The child wanders around quietly, thinking of all the things they can do without Mommy telling them *no*. But it's just a matter of time, seconds usually, before they realize they don't want to do it alone. They need buddies to cause the most mischief. And so like a coyote during a full moon, they search for their pack. One child quickly becomes three.

All awake.

Causing trouble.

The thought of it makes me sick.

I'm not sure how it happened. They just appeared one day. I remember having my first child: the sleepless nights caring for him, the first time he crawled, his first steps. And then something strange happened, as if I'd walked through the Bermuda Triangle, although I'm pretty sure I've never been there before.

All I know is I woke up one day with four children (though sometimes I swear there are more). At first I thought I was just babysitting, but when parents never came to pick the kids up, it dawned on me that they might be mine.

I slowly look to my alarm clock that has yet to go off. I'm already cringing before I see the time—6:10 a.m. I want to bang my head into the headboard and would too, if I wasn't so tired. I don't want a day like this. I haven't had a chance to recover from the last crazy day. *Yesterday.*

I close my eyes and focus my hearing. Maybe the child will return to bed. I pray for this, but experience has taught me that this prayer is usually ignored.

It's not long before I hear the patter of feet. The sound is faint, but it's there. Several of them. I hear the TV in the living room click on. I debate whether or not to make them all go back to sleep. As if that were possible. But if I let them stay awake, then I know by 5:00 this afternoon, I will have three very cranky kids.

I listen to my husband breathe heavily, deep in sleep. He hadn't heard the house come alive like I had. Years ago I would've woken him to suffer with me, but I've toughened up since then. There's very little I can't handle now.

Of course, the day has just begun.

I swing my legs from the bed and sit up. My reflection in the full-length mirror across from me makes me want to bury myself back into the blankets. My hair has medusasized and my forehead sports a deep imprint of the zipper from my body pillow case. I rub it and the sleep from my eyes, but when I hear kids burst into laughter, I jump up. The last thing I need is for Baby to wake up early too.

Poor Baby. My last child. I'm not sure how old he is, and I can't remember his name (I'm pretty much brain-dead by now). I do know he's still in diapers and can speak one word, "Mama." His eyes are this crazy electric-blue color, making me think that once a month he turns into a wolf. That might explain his aggressive behavior toward others. I definitely don't want him waking up too early.

"What are you guys doing awake?" I ask as I shuffle into the living room. All three older kids sit huddled together on the sofa.

Grant, my eight-year-old, turns to me. "I couldn't sleep."

"So why are Sydney and Ashlyn awake?"

Grant's gaze returns to the lit up television. The light reflects in his bright blue eyes.

"Grant?"

"They couldn't sleep either."

"Really?"

"Mom, my homework's done and by the door on top of my backpack, but you need to sign it," my six-year-old Sydney says. She's the most organized kid I know and has been waiting over a year for the County Courthouse to approve her business licenses for a daycare, a grocery store, an animal hospital, and a day spa.

I'm still looking at Grant. "I will. Just remind me before you leave for school." I step in front of Grant, forcing him to look at me. "If you get up early, are you supposed to wake up the girls?"

His mouth drops open. "But they wanted me to!"

"And you know this how?"

He waves his hands toward the girls. "Ask them."

This conversation was going nowhere. "Whatever, just don't do it again. And make sure everyone's quiet. I don't want Baby to wake up."

He nods, then cranks his head to the side to see the TV behind me.

"Mom?" Ashlyn's soft voice asks. At four years old, she's as tall as Sydney.

I look at her.

"Mom?" she says again.

I'm still looking. Directly into her green eyes.

"Mom?"

"Ashlyn, I'm looking right at you."

"You have to say 'what'."

I inhale deeply. "What?"

"Can I have a bath?"

I look at the time and then at her. Her blonde hair is worse than mine, and I think I see food in it from the night before. "Sure, but let's be quiet." I glance over at Sydney. She looks almost as bad as Ashlyn. "Why don't you guys take one together."

"Can I bring in some toys?" Ashlyn says.

"Yes, but they have to be water toys."

"Yay!" She smiles and runs into the kitchen. I hear a drawer open.

"What are you doing?" I ask.

"Getting toys." She runs past me holding a spatula, ladle, ice cream scoop, and a cup. More dishes to wash later. Add it the mountain of laundry. I turn to Grant. "You could probably use a bath too."

"I'm good," he says.

I smell his hair. "Your stench would suggest otherwise. Go get in the shower. And don't take forever."

I walk into the girls' bathroom. They are already naked and sitting in an empty tub, even though water pours from the faucet.

"It's not filling," Ashlyn says.

I bend over and pull the drain stopper. "That should help." I return to the living room where Grant still watches TV. I walk over to it and shut it off. "Get in the shower right now."

He mumbles something, but I don't want to know what.

Back in the kitchen, I begin to make pancakes. Measure. Pour. Mix. The girls are arguing in the bathroom, but I resist the urge to intervene. The frying pan warms up, and I pour my first three pancakes. I open a drawer and search for a spatula but find none. I turn to the sink. A spatula caked in dried scrambled eggs lies on top of a pile of dishes.

I return to the bathroom. "Ashlyn, I need my spatula back."

She quickly hides it beneath her—sitting on it with her bare bum. "What spatula?"

"Come on! That's disgusting," I say. "Give it back to me."

"I don't know what you're talking about." She smiles, and Sydney giggles.

"I'm serious. I'll count to three."

Her eyes shift to Sydney for support. Sydney looks just as hesitant as Ashlyn.

"One."

Ashlyn's concerned thoughts seem to visibly float into the air. "Is she bluffing?" they say.

"Two." I lean over.

I'm about to say three when she quickly reaches beneath her and tosses the spatula (along with a spray of water) in my direction. "Just teasing! It's right here!"

I dry my face while trying to remain calm. "Please hurry," I say. "And don't forget to wash your hair." I exit the bathroom and walk into the hall when my nose is accosted by a rank smell. *Barf.* Unwillingly, I inhale again, but this time I smell nothing. Odd.

In the kitchen smoke rises from my griddle. *Shoot!* Not having time to wash the spatula, I quickly slide it under the pancakes and flip them over. They are as black as the scuff marks on my kitchen floor. I almost decide to keep them, thinking I can trick the kids by hiding their bad side, and then mask the taste by dousing them with whip cream, but when I check the fridge and realize I'm out of cream, I toss the pancakes and start over.

"Hurry up, kids!" I call, hoping they can hear me. I quickly set the table, even cutting up an orange and placing a section onto each plate. *I'm really outdoing myself today*, I think and smile. But the smile disappears when I see the time.

"Girls! Come on, it's time!" I walk back to their room to make sure I'm being listened to when again the sour smell of vomit punches me in the face. I sniff around but can't seem to find its location. The funky smell seems to be floating through my house, haunting me. A nasty-smelling poltergeist. Just what I need.

I stick my head into the girls' bathroom. Thankfully, I don't have to yell, although my lungs have already expanded to do just that. Both girls are out of the tub and drying off. I exhale and say, "You don't have much time. Please hurry and get dressed and then come eat. Got it?"

They nod, but I don't see their eyes. "Both of you look at me." Their gazes find mine. "I mean it. No playing. No messing around. Get dressed and come eat. Okay?"

"Got it," they say.

I knock on the other bathroom door. "Grant?"

"Yeah?" The water's still running.

"You need to get out now. Breakfast's on the table."

"K."

I wait a second expecting some sort of an argument, but when it doesn't come, I return to the kitchen.

And wait.

I tap my foot.

I notice grime caked around my kitchen sink faucet.

I read the back of the pancake mix: 250 calories per pancake. I pretend I don't see the zero.

I stand up to yell, when, as if the kids had been testing my patience, they appear at the same time fully dressed. "You guys are going to have to eat fast," I say.

Sydney and Ashlyn pull up a chair and reach for the pancakes. Grant remains standing.

"What's up?" I ask.

"Can I just have one of your shakes?"

"No. They're my diet shakes, and they cost a lot of money."

"But I don't want pancakes."

"I don't care. This is breakfast."

"Can I eat at school?"

"No. I made a nice meal, now please sit down and eat."

He scowls and jerks a chair out from the table. The legs scrape against the wood floor. "Chill out, Grant," I warn as I make the rounds, helping each kid with their food.

"Did you sign my homework?" Sydney asks.

"Not yet."

Her eyes grow big. "But, Mom, I need it! If I don't have it back at exactly 8:30, I won't get a star."

"I know. I'll get to it. One thing at a time." I glance at the clock, thinking I may have a quick minute to eat too. I place a couple of pancakes on my plate when barf ghost tickles my nose again. "Can you guys smell that?"

They all sniff. "Smell what?"

I sniff again, but it's gone. "Never mind."

After setting up the perfect pancake stack with just the right amount of real butter layered with rivers of warm syrup, I lift my fork to take a bite.

"Mom!" Sydney yells suddenly.

I jump and my small piece of heaven slides off the fork and onto my lap. My worn pajama bottoms absorb the sticky syrup. "What do you want, Sydney?" I snap.

"My hair!" She grabs at it as if she's going to rip it out. "It's not done. What am I going to do?"

"Calm down. Take a few more bites, and then we'll do it."

In the bathroom once more, I take a towel and try to dry her thick hair. "There's no time," I say and frown.

Sydney frowns. "Another ponytail?"

"Sure." Poor Sydney. Most daughters have their hair done in six ponytails all twisted in roses and tulips, pinned up high on their head. And then there's my daughter. Always sporting a barely tight ponytail that hangs like the back end of a shaggy mutt.

"Ouch!" Sydney says and moves her head away from the brush in my hand.

"I'm barely brushing it."

She touches the back of her head. "You're ripping it out! Am I bleeding?"

"Do you see any clumps of hair or blood anywhere? Now hold still. You're going to miss the bus if we can't get this done."

She crosses her arms and almost her eyebrows.

I try to brush her wet hair as gently as possible, but time is against me. In less than a minute I have a badly made ponytail and a very mad little girl. "All done," I say. "Now go finish eating, then get your coat and backpack on." She stomps off. I try not to stomp after her.

Back in the kitchen, I find Grant missing, and he still has over half of his pancake left. "Grant?"

No answer.

I turn to Ashlyn who's sitting quietly at the table, rearranging her pancake pieces with her fingers. I ignore the syrup dripping off her fingers and onto her shirt and ask, "Where's Grant?"

She stares right through me.

"Ashlyn, where's Grant?"

"You know what I want for Christmas?" she says. "That shiny thing with the purple buttons. Can you get it for me?"

I shake my head and walk off. "Grant?" I call down the stairs.

Nothing.

I'm about to storm downstairs when Grant suddenly comes in from the garage and slams the door. "Grant!" I shout. "You'll wake the baby!"

Just like Ashlyn, he doesn't hear me. His face is red and he's breathing heavily. "I can't find my homework! And I've looked everywhere!"

I close my eyes and imagine he's said something incredibly sweet and calm, like "My backpack's ready, I've brushed my teeth, and I even have two minutes to spare to help you clear off the table."

Grant waves his hands in front of my face. "Mom! Are you listening? I can't find my homework!"

I look down at him. "Did you look in your room?"

"Yes."

"Did you look in my office?"

"Yes."

"Did you look in your pant pockets?"

"Yes."

"Did you look in the car?"

"Yes."

"Did you look in the toy box?"

"Twice."

I frown. "Then I don't know what to tell you." I walk to my room. "I'm going to watch out the window," I say over my shoulder. From our back window we have a great view to the road behind us to check for the bus before it rounds the corner to our house.

"But what about my homework?" Grant cries, following after me.

I peer out the window. "Tell her your dog ate it," I mumble.

"We don't have a dog," Grant says.

I ignore the snootiness in his voice. "Then tell her your tarantula ate it. That's more believable."

Grant throws up his hands. "I hate today!" He takes his jacket and stuffs it into his backpack.

"It's cold outside. You should probably put that on," I tell him.

"I'd rather freeze."

I spot the welcoming yellow bus lumbering up the street behind our home. I almost weep at its presence and take a small, precious moment, before I say, "Bus is here!"

Panic ensues, filling the air with chaotic shouts, and it doesn't come alone. It's partnered with my stinky poltergeist, who's suddenly back to torment me.

"You haven't signed my homework!" Sydney cries, bursting into tears.

"I need a cold lunch," Grant yells.

Ashlyn's tugging on my shirt. "And then I want the doll that pees, and the sandy art thing, and the pink—"

"Everybody quiet!" I shout.

I take hold of a crayon on the floor and sign Sydney's homework, then say, "Grant, you'll have to eat hot lunch today. I didn't have time to make you a cold one."

"But we're having weenie boats!" he cries.

Whether it's the sudden sharpness of his voice, cutting the last of my sanity, or the vomit ghost climbing up my nose, I snap. I grab Grant by the shoulders, and inches from his face, say "You will eat your weenie boats and you will like it. And when you come home you will search for your homework or you're grounded for a month!"

"Oh, and Mom?" Ashlyn says. "I also want a puppy."

I turn to Ashlyn, possessed. "That's not going to happen, you want to know why?" Her eyes slowly grow big. "Because Santa's not—"

"Don't do it, Mom!" Grant says, stepping between us.

I straighten up and take a deep breath.

"Mom, we have to go!" Sydney's hand is on the doorknob.

I roll my shoulders back. "Not without a hug," I say and embrace them tightly. "Things will be better when you come home. Mommy will be better," I promise.

They leave looking miserable. I wave good-bye, but they don't reciprocate it. Both of them are still upset, and I don't blame them. I feel horrible for loosing my temper. Why did some higher power ever think I could be a mom?

"Mommy?"

I turn to Ashlyn.

"Does Santa like me?"

I get down on my knees in front of her. "Of course he does. I was just being a meanie. Sometimes I say things because I'm frustrated, but I don't really mean them. Do you want to watch the kids walk to the bus stop?"

She nods.

"Good." I lift her up and she giggles as I spin her around the room and plop her on the couch in front of the window. I relax into the sofa, feeling better now that the morning is over.

Ashlyn points. "Mommy, Grant and Sydney are fighting."

"Huh?" I look out the window. Sure enough both kids are shoving. Behind them the bus rolls closer, but they don't see it. I bolt for the door and run outside onto the porch. "Stop fighting," I scream. "The bus is right there!"

The kids freeze and then slowly turn around. I know their thoughts when they see the bus. They're wondering if they can make it. I yell again, and they start running. Grant's faster so he makes it there first. Sydney, however, decides to give up, and stops halfway. My face suddenly feels like the flaming morning sun. "Run, Sydney!" I scream. "Run!"

Hearing my voice reach an unimaginable octave spurs her into action. She sprints toward Grant (or away from me), barely making it to the bus as the doors open.

I wait until I see both kids disappear into my favorite vehicle before I return inside and slump to the floor, my back against the closed front door.

"What's wrong, Mommy?" Ashlyn asks.

I shake my head. "It's been a long day is all."

She smooths my hair. "But it's only morning."

I flop my head back. I'm about to say "I know," when the smelly poltergeist returns. "What *is* that?" I say.

"What?"

I stand up. "Do you smell it?" I ask.

Ashlyn holds my hand and nods. "It's stinky."

I walk around the house sniffing. The smell grows stronger the closer I come to Baby's room.

"It's Baby," I whisper.

"It's really stinky here," Ashlyn says, holding her nose in front of the door.

I place my hand on the doorknob, heart pounding. I'm terrified of what I'm about to discover. Just beyond the door, I hear Baby coo. The sound is deep and throaty, almost threatening. A monster. A terrible, smelly monster.

I push Ashlyn forward. "You first."

She stares at me, shocked.

"Fine, I'll go," I say.

I open the door and am blasted by a horrendous, gut-wrenching smell. But that's not what makes me want to drop to the floor in the fetal position, thumb shoved in my mouth; it's the sight of my child.

He's standing in his crib, wide eyed. I notice his eyes first because it's all I recognize of my once somewhat-handsome boy. The rest of him is covered in vomit. I'm amazed at the amount of throw up, not only on him, but inside his crib as well. His whole mattress is covered by a thick, pinkish, chunky goo. Parts of it have crumbled off and found their way to the carpet in what looks like an escape attempt.

But that's not all.

Baby has finger painted last nights dinner on the walls. Cave man drawings of a severely disturbed child.

"Mama," he says and smiles.

I shake my head. "Don't call me that. Don't ever call me that again."

"Mama! Mama!" He slaps his hands on the crib's wooden rail, splattering throw up in all directions.

The gravity of the situation hits me, and in my mind I imagine myself collapsing to my knees, arms out stretched. A torturous cry resembling those of dying soldiers left lying on the battle field rips from my lungs. "Noooooooo!" But instead I only whimper like an injured animal and limp away to turn on the bath water.

"Mama! Mama!" Baby cries after me.

I pretend I don't hear him and sit on the side of the tub while it fills.

"Mama! Mama!"

"He really wants you, Mom," Ashlyn says in a tight nasal voice. She's still plugging her nose.

I can only nod.

When the tub is half empty (nothing is half full today), I shut off the water and return to Baby's room. I stare at the mess again wondering how in the world I am going to clean it all without a zookeeper's elephant hose.

The first thing I do is open the window. After taking a deep breath of the cool morning air, I turn to Baby. Smiling, I say, "Touchdown!" Baby raises his arms, and I quickly pull his shirt over his head. The front of it smears even more barf onto his face; a chunk of what looks like a pink chicken nugget sticks to his cheek.

Now comes the tricky part.

His pajama bottoms.

In addition to the vomit crisis, Baby has also peed his pants and the new generic brand of diapers I bought the other day clearly couldn't contain his super urine. I begin carefully, inching down the side of his pants while also trying to avoid his smelly grasp, but this proves difficult seeing how he's inside a crib. Our movements become like some kind of ancient Chinese ninja dance. I dive in and pull.

Baby reaches.

I duck and lunge forward.

Pull.

Baby claws.

I duck, lunge again until I have his pants around his ankles.

Now what?

My ninja dance won't work for what needs to be done next.

"You're going to have to pick him up," Ashlyn says from the door.

"You pick him up."

She grunts. "But I'm too little!"

"I'll get the ladder."

"I have to pee." She runs away.

Ashlyn's right. I know it. There are no other options. Unless . . .

"I love you, Baby," I say, smiling big. Do you think you can do mommy a favor?"

He stares.

"Can you take your pants off?"

He slaps his hand on the wooden rail.

"Come on. Take your pants off." I point to them. "You can do it! Stomp your feet!"

I stomp my feet, smiling and looking like I'm having the time of my life while I chant:

"Stomp your feet, stomp your feet,

Don't miss a beat, and stomp your feet.

You smell real bad, you look real gross.

So move those legs, and stomp those toes!"

I stop moving, panting, but am still smiling.

And he's still staring.

Nothing. I frown and slump my shoulders. I'd hoped my child was smart enough to understand what I'm saying, but clearly he inherited his father's genes.

I square my shoulders. "Let's do this," I say and dive in without thinking. I reach under his slimy armpits and lift. It's then I realize my mistake: I haven't contained his hands. His fingers connect with my face, smearing barf all over.

I keep my mouth closed and scream, "MMMMMMMM!" as I can feel a chunk of something on my lip. I quickly jiggle Baby until his pants fall off and then dash into the hall and into the bathroom.

As soon as Baby's standing in the tub, I unlatch his diaper and step back. Baby sits down happy as can be. That makes one of us. I whip around, turn on the bathroom sink, and squish my whole head under it.

And scrub.

I lift my wet face and stare at myself in the mirror. The eyes of a warrior return my glare. James Dooley music begins to play in my head, and I imagine myself smearing black paint in a pattern across my face. *This Baby is mine.*

"Mama!" Baby cries.

"You say something, kid?" I turn around slowly.

He tilts his head and stares as if he doesn't recognize me.

I smile. "Yeah, that's right. I'm in control. Who's your mommy now?"

His eyebrows raise, and I know in that moment he's regretting ever leaving my womb. I attack him head on. Cups of water rain down on him, while my free hand scrubs off the caked-on barf. While still scrubbing, I drain the water, forcing larger barf wads down the drain with the end of the toilet plunger. I then refill the tub and bathe Baby all over again. At first he laughs, thinking that me twisting him up, down, and around is some sort of game, but by the end he looks woozy, so I slow down for fear he might throw up again. The whole process takes less than two minutes, which I'm convinced would make it into *The Guinness World Book of Records* if they had such a category.

Baby's dressed and sitting in his highchair, chewing on a piece of bread. I'm afraid to give him anything else, especially if it's colored. "Keep an eye on him, Ashlyn," I say. She mumbles an "okay" through a bite full of pancake.

Now comes the tough part.

Beneath the kitchen sink I find a pair of yellow rubber gloves, in my bedroom closet I throw on a robe, and in Grant's toy box I steal a Halloween monster mask with long hair and blood stains on its white face. Sufficiently covered from head to foot, I stand at my Baby's door holding a bottle of the strongest cleaner I could find and a handful of rags in my other. Then I attack.

I start with the walls, then strip the bed, shoving the sheets into a heavy duty garbage bag. I'm not even going to bother washing them. Finally all that's left is the crib and mattress. The mattress cleans easily enough, but the old wooden rails have absorbed the stomach bile like a sponge. I can't scrub it enough. Too many cracks and crevices. Minutes later, I give up. There's nothing else I can do.

The room still smells terrible, but I can only hope that the fresh air from the open window will be enough to combat it.

"Mama!" Baby yells from the kitchen. "Mamaaaaaaaaaa!"

His terrible screech tightens my nerves. I hurry back to him and discover he has attempted to get out from his high chair and is stuck, one leg on the tray and the other jammed beneath it. I'm half tempted to let him stay there; it doesn't look like he can go anywhere.

As if he can sense my thoughts, he cries again. "Mamaaaaaaaaa!"

"Argh! I'm right here, kid!" I remove the tray and then

him. He toddles off to an unknown location. As long as the bathroom doors are closed, I don't care where.

Ashlyn turns on the TV. "All cleaned up?" she says.

"Yes, finally."

She stretches out on the couch. "Good, 'cause I've had a rough morning, and I just want to relax. Think you can keep it down?"

4

The Community Swimming Pool

They appear out of nowhere. A planned attack, no doubt. They've learned at an early age that battles are won in numbers. I step away from my four children, including Baby, whose face looks innocent enough, but he is with *them*.

"Mom," Grant says as he takes a step toward me. "We want to go—," the next word that falls from his round, wet lips is one I dread the most—"swimming."

"You want to go trimming?" I say, praying I heard wrong.

"Swimming," he repeats.

"Yeah. We want to go swimming," Sydney chimes in.

I turn around to continue washing dishes. Maybe if I ignore them, they'll get bored and walk away. Wait—was that dogs or children?

"Mommy, take us swimming!" Ashlyn shouts.

All of a sudden, I'm like an old lady sitting on a park bench surrounded by pigeons but holding an empty bread bag.

"Swimming." One nudges my leg.

"Swimming." Another pulls my shirt.

"Swimming." This one steps on my foot.

The last one burps.

My resolve crumbles. I sigh. "So you guys want to go swimming?"

"Yeah!" they chorus.

"Will you be good?"

They nod.

"Promise?"

Nods again, but their eyes look elsewhere.

"All right. Go get ready. And remember to pack a towel and a change of underwear." They flutter away.

Carrying Baby, I reluctantly walk into my bedroom. My heart begins to pound and sweat pools in my pits as I come face to face with *the drawer*. I blow a thick layer of dust off its handle and stare. "What do you think, Baby? Will I find one that fits?"

He barfs down the front of his shirt.

"My sentiments exactly."

After mumbling a few words of encouragement to myself, I open the drawer. I am familiar with all of its contents, but comfortable with none of them: two short nighties, a bustier top, stockings with only one matching garter belt (the other belt had been used to tighten a Halloween costume for one of my children years ago), and an assortment of swimsuits.

I remove the swimsuit I use the most—a blue and green tie-dye one given to me by my sister in the eighties. The material is thin and the bum area so threadbare I can practically see through it. But it fits.

I hand the swimsuit to Baby and continue to rummage through the rest of the items: an unused sports bra, a floral grandma swimsuit with a skirt (a gift from my mom), and a bikini—this one I should burn.

"I guess this will have to do," I say and wrestle the tie-dye swimsuit away from Baby.

After pulling on the stretchy material, I look at myself in the mirror. Where there should be hills, I have valleys, and where there should be valleys, I have mountains. Just then I remember a conversation I'd overheard between two farmers at church last Sunday. One had said he could fix anything with duct tape. I stick my head out the door. "Grant!"

"Yeah, Mom?" he calls back from downstairs.

"Do you know where dad's duct tape is?"

"I used it all on my fort. Why?"

"No reason." I frown and close the door. On to the next best thing. I grab one of my husband's tank tops and pull it over the swimsuit. There. Mission accomplished—sort of.

Baby claps.

I open the bedroom door and yell to anyone listening, "Load up, kids!"

In one arm, I carry a diaper bag, purse, and backpack full of towels. In the other, I hold Baby and trudge to the family SUV. I try not to, but I stop and scowl at the large black beast, perched high on four oversized wheels. Every day I wish for a minivan—one with two sliding doors that open with a touch of a button, easy access to the rear seats, and, of course, built-in DVD player. Instead, I'm stuck with a jacked-up hunting rig. My husband thinks converting to a minivan would kill off the last of his masculinity. His masculinity used to mean something to me too, but now all I care about is folding rear seats and onboard entertainment.

"Grant!" I snap, when I see him shove his sisters out of the way and yank the door open. "Ladies first!" But he is already inside and scrambling over the seat to sit in the back. The girls climb in after him, all the while fighting over who gets to sit in the middle. Ashlyn's voice is the loudest so she wins.

"You can sit there on the way home," I promise Sydney.

The kids are quiet as I drive away, and I relax into the seat, but the second I pull out of the driveway, they begin to argue. I close my eyes and imagine I'm in the bathroom—the last sanctuary in my home.

Then the screams begin—blood-curdling cries, each one louder than the one before. "Mine was way louder than yours!" Sydney yells.

"Aaahhhh!" Ashlyn shouts, followed by a roar from Grant.

I glance at my children in the rearview mirror. I know their names, but at the moment I can remember none of them. "Would you please *be quiet*?" I shout, winning the screaming contest. They look at one another and giggle, but at least they're quiet.

After too many minutes, the community swimming pool finally comes into view. It's a scary sight. The round dome, once painted white, is a dark rust color, and the brick exterior makes it look more like a prison than a friendly community pool. I can practically hear it groan at our presence. I groan right back.

I help the kids out of the car and remind them not to trip on the uneven sidewalk. Most of them listen, but the broken-up concrete snags Ashlyn's little shoe and she falls face first. A cry, resembling the sound I imagine a pterodactyl makes, tears from her lungs. I drop everything in my arms, except for Baby, and try to comfort her. "It will stop hurting when the pain goes away," I tell her, but she isn't listening. She finally stops crying when I promise a trip to the dollar store later. Another stressful adventure.

After I give my hard-earned cash to the black-haired, eyebrow-pierced teenager behind the counter, I send Grant to the men's locker room to change and take the other kids into the women's dressing room. "Let's get undressed over here," I say and guide the girls into a corner stall. I try to pull the curtain shut, but it stops halfway. Really? I try three more stalls until I find one with a curtain wide enough to give us some privacy. No one needs to see my lightning bolt-sized stretch marks.

With Baby tucked under my arm like a football, I use my free hand to help the girls pull off their clothes. But when it's time for me to get undressed, I wonder aloud what to do with the Baby.

"Just set him down," Sydney says.

I look down at the wet, brown-tiled floor. A murky foam sizzles on top, snapping and popping like an escaped science experiment. Afraid for my Baby's life, I continue to hold him while I miraculously undress.

"Let's go, Mommy!" the girls complain.

"I'm almost ready." Hopping on one foot, Baby's head bobbing up and down, I remove my second sock. I quickly slip my feet into flip-flops before the foam creature can attach itself to my skin. "Done. Let's go."

I herd the kids out of the dressing room and find Grant waiting impatiently outside.

"You guys took forever!" he says and then dashes off toward the pool, followed by his sisters.

I'm the last to get in as I keep expecting the lifeguard to stop me for practically wearing street clothes into the pool, but he's busy staring at a woman standing on the diving board. She has a perfectly sculpted body, untouched by the cruel hands of pregnancy. I want to stare too, but just then Baby spits up in the water. I quickly push the barf away to be blamed on someone else.

Gingerly, I manage to submerge myself and Baby waist-deep into the water without having a heart attack from the cold. Apparently, warm water is a luxury a community swimming pool can't afford.

A neighbor friend spots me and says hello just as Ashlyn appears from the chlorinated depths and suddenly yanks the tank top and the front of my swimsuit down with incredible strength. "Mommy! I want to go down the slide!" she wails.

I quickly pull my clothing back up before my neighbor has me arrested for indecent exposure. "Fine. Go."

"Can you come with me?"

"I can't. I'm holding the baby, but I'll watch."

Ashlyn swipes her tongue all around her lips and stares at the four-foot red slide as if it were a giant dinosaur.

I take hold of her hand. "You can do it. I promise. I'll be waiting for you at the bottom."

Attempt number one.

She looks to me and then to the slide. With the courage of a knight, she lets go of my hand and bobs to the edge of the pool. And bobs right back.

"Come on, sweetie. Really, it's not scary," I say.

Attempt number two.

I walk with her to the edge of the pool and gently encourage her to get out. She stands on the edge, water dripping from a saggy swimsuit and then dives back into the water.

Attempt number three.

I hold her hand as she gets out of the pool and, while I'm still in the water, I pull her forward to the slide. Her upper body freezes, while I'm still pulling, and she falls on her bum and begins to cry. I hold her and Baby.

Attempt number four.

I beg, she cries.

Attempt number five.

After handing Baby to my friend, I find myself sitting on top of the slide, hips crammed between its edges, and Ashlyn on my lap. I decide to take advantage of the moment and use it as a learning tool to explain how to go down a slide properly. "You must always lean forward, otherwise you'll fall back and smack your head. Get ready! Lean forward. Go!"

It's then that I realize I'm top heavy—funny, because I swear I'm bottom heavy. I fall back, legs flipping into the air, and Ashlyn into my chest. My head crashes against the hard plastic slide loud enough to give everyone pause. I splash into the pool, wishing desperately I were a mermaid. I'd swim to the deep end and hide in shame. But there was no King Titan around to grant my wish; only my three-year-old who's trying frantically to find solid ground, and my face beneath her foot isn't helping.

"Was that fun?" I ask when I pop out of the water, acting natural so everyone thinks I meant to do that.

"Yeah! Can we do it again?"

I shake my head. "Not me. Mommy has a headache, but I'll bet you can do it all by yourself."

This time she doesn't hesitate. She marches to the slide and zips down expertly. So much like a pro that I wonder if I'd just been played.

I retrieve Baby and glance around for my two oldest kids. Grant has found a friend from school and is jumping off the diving board, and Sydney is in the corner of the pool, chewing on something. I make my way to her. "What are you eating?"

She looks up at me, eyes blank. "Huh?"

"You're chewing on something. What is it?"

She reaches into her mouth and pulls it out. "It went into my mouth when I was swimming." She drops it into my hand.

I look at it closely. Bile rises in my throat when I realize what it is.

Sydney peers over my hand. "Hey! Is that a Band-Aid?"

I shudder and quickly toss it into the pool's gutter. "Ten more minutes, and then we're out of here." *I can hold on for ten more minutes*, I tell myself.

Gratefully time flies as I'm preoccupied trying to keep an eye on everyone. Finally, after three more warnings, I manage to get the kids out of the pool and into the dressing room.

"Aren't you going to change?" Sydney asks.

I stare at the cesspool at the bottom of the stall. Do I really need another wart on my foot? "No, let's just go."

Fortunately, we make it home with no incidents. Mostly because the kids have all swallowed too much chlorinated water and aren't feeling very well. Their noses are red and eyes bloodshot, but I know their groggy state will only last for twenty more minutes. This might give me enough time to make it inside my house and enjoy a chocolate chip cookie and milk uninterrupted. This thought makes me press on the gas pedal.

At home, I unload the children and rush them inside. "Why don't you guys turn on the TV and watch a cartoon for a few minutes?" I say, and then disappear into the kitchen. I remove the milk from the fridge and turn around.

There they are. All four of them. Again. Staring. But this time I'm more prepared. I square my shoulders and lift my chin. I won't be beaten this time. "Yes?" I say.

"We just want to tell you that you're the best mom in the whole world," Grant says.

"Yeah. Totally the nicest and the coolest," Sydney adds.

"You're pretty, Mommy." Ashlyn grins.

Baby giggles, then drools.

I let out my breath and smile. "You guys are awesome too. Did you have fun today?"

They cheer in agreement. "Maybe we can do it again soon?" Grant asks.

I look down at my children's angelic faces. And in that moment, just like a new mother who's forgotten the pregnancy pains of nine—make that ten—months, I see only the joy they've given me. "Of course," I say and give them all a great big hug.

5

Heed the Warnings

God gave me plenty of warnings to stop my journey well before it began. I wish I would've listened, but just like my children, I am slow to learn. It started with Sydney's missing shoe. Actually, it started with me thinking that taking four kids on a bike ride was a good idea. But I missed the first warning just like I missed the second.

We are all ready to go except for Sydney who is circling her room, searching for her other pink tennis shoe. "I can't find it!" she shouts. "Someone took it!"

I hold Baby on my lap and offer him his sippy cup. "We're not leaving until you find it," I say, keeping my voice even.

She stomps into the living room. "Can't I just wear my cleats?"

Baby pushes the cup away. "No. You need to wear tennis shoes," I tell her. I don't really care that she wears her cleats, but I'm trying to teach her a lesson. A six-year-old should be able to keep track of her shoes, right? "You need to actually look, Sydney. Here—" I pretend to pluck my eyes from my sockets and hand them to her. "Use my mom eyes and see if they can find them."

Sydney snorts and drops my invisible eyes to the ground. "Can I wear my boots?"

"No," I say, more firmly. "Where did you find your other tennis shoe?"

"Downstairs."

"Then the other one is there, too. That's what's great about shoes. They're very loyal to each other."

"What does that mean?"

I shift Baby in my arms. He's squirming like crazy, refusing to drink. "Nothing. Just go downstairs and look for it. Really look. Lift up blankets, move things around. Just look!"

She throws her arms into the air and struts away. Each step is short and loud, making me think of a snare drum.

"And if you can't find it in five minutes, then we're not going!" I call after her.

An angry sigh rushes up from downstairs. I turn my attention to the other two children who are watching television. "Grant and Ashlyn, if you want to go on a bike ride, then you better help Sydney find her shoe." My words are snuffed out by a high-pitched voice of Disney character who's having a bizarre meltdown on the TV. I pick up the remote and click "power." It takes a moment for the kids to realize they're staring at a black screen. "Go downstairs and help Sydney find her shoe! Now!"

Another warning comes when I don't stand by my original warning to Sydney. Five minutes pass and the kids still haven't found the shoe, and I'm still telling them to find it. Finally, the shoe appears. I'm the one who finds it stuffed beneath Grant's dirty shirt, the same shirt I asked him to pick up earlier that morning. It's been ten minutes, but I still decide to continue the journey.

And everyone's happy.

But we quickly discover all but one of the tires are flat. Grant's bike tires aren't just flat; they've been popped.

I should've stopped right then.

End the whole trip.

Do something else.

Reduce my stress.

But I don't.

I want my kids to have a fun, and I'm bound to make it happen, come hell or high water.

Because of Grant's tire, he wants to take his rollerblades instead.

"You're going to get tired," I say.

He looks at me like I'm the biggest moron in the world. "It's my feet on wheels. How am I going to get tired?"

"Whatever. Let's just go."

Our bike ride begins easily enough, despite the ominous feeling growing in my gut. I stand to pedal up a small hill before we reach the bike path. Pulling two kids behind me in a bike carrier is harder than I expect. Or it's been so long since I've exercised that my muscles have atrophied.

Sydney rides in the lead, racing far enough ahead that I have to constantly remind her to slow down. Grant brings up the rear; his rollerblades proving not to be as effective as he hoped, but he manages to keep up. Just barely.

At first, the ride is smooth, but it's not long before I notice the bike becoming harder to control. I feel as if I'm being pulled backward and am quickly losing control. I glance behind me to discover the source of the problem. Grant is hanging onto the back of the carriage, hunched over is if to avoid detection.

"Let go," I say.

He shakes his head.

"Let go!"

"No way. My legs are tired." He's refusing to look at me.

"Grant, I can't control the bike when you're hanging on."

"So what am I supposed to do? Let my legs fall off?"

I face forward and consider my options. We're about a half a mile from home. I could stop our trip, turn us all around and make him walk home. (At the last second, I'd made Grant put his tennis shoes into the carriage—the only smart decision of the whole trip.) The kids will be mad, which in turn will make me mad.

Or.

I can make it work.

"Fine. Just hang on and don't wiggle," I say, settling into my seat for the long haul.

Baby starts crying again. "What's wrong with him?" I ask Ashlyn.

"I don't know."

"Give him his milk."

"That's what I'm doing, but he keeps throwing it."

Just then I notice Sydney way ahead of us and about to cross the bridge over the river. "Sydney!" I yell. "Stop!" She waits a full minute before we catch up to her.

"Can we walk to the river?" she asks, motioning her head toward the water.

I look hesitantly to the wide, yet calm, waters. "All right. Park your bikes off the trail. Grant, put your shoes on." It takes just a second to remove Ashlyn and the baby from the bike carrier. Baby, who's just learned to walk, seems especially eager. His blue eyes are as big as a crystal ball, the river reflects in their glossy surface.

"Be careful!" I call to the older children as they carefully make their way across a sea of river rock.

When I catch up to them, I notice Grant's frowning. "What's wrong?"

Grant points. "I want to get to the big river."

I see what he means. In front of us is a small finger-like appendage to the river that has branched off. The stream blocks our path from reaching the bigger section.

"Please, Mom? Can I cross?" he asks.

I tighten my grip on Baby's hand as he's fighting desperately to be free. "I don't want anyone's shoes getting wet."

"They won't. I can jump."

"You can't jump that far."

"Yes I can. I did it with Dad last week." He crosses his arms.

"Well the water wasn't this high then."

"So? I can still do it."

"No you can't."

"Uh-huh."

"Serious. You can't make that."

"You wanna bet?"

Why am I arguing with a nine-year-old? "Grant, there's no way you can make it. But we can throw in some big rocks for you to cross on."

The kids like this idea and begin to toss every rock they touch into the water. I even encourage Baby to try, but he's not interested. All he cares about is walking straight into the water. I pick him up, tucking him like a football, and then toss the largest river rocks I can find.

"You made a bridge, Mommy!" Ashlyn says.

I tilt my head. "Sort of."

"Here I go!" Grant says.

He takes his first step successfully, balancing on one foot, arms outstretched, but when he leaps to the next rock as graceful as a hippo, his foot slips. "What do I do?" he shouts. Both feet are emerged into six inches of water.

I groan. "You might as well keep going. You're shoes are already wet."

He stomps his hippo legs the rest of the way. By the time he's on the other side, his pants are soaking wet too.

"Don't go too far!" I say.

He waves and takes off to get a closer look at the river.

"Can I go too, Mom?" Sydney asks.

"No, but maybe next time if I don't have the baby. Then I can help you cross."

For the next few minutes, I let the girls throw rocks into the little stream while I hold tightly to Baby as he dips his chubby fingers into the water. Every few seconds, I look up to make sure I can still see Grant's head bobbing just over a rise. When I look up again, I realize I can't see him.

"Grant!" I yell and begin to pace the creek's edge. "Grant!" I'm about to dart across the stream when Grant finally appears.

"Mom, I caught a fish!" he says, walking toward me.

"No you didn't. And stay where I can see you."

"Yes, I did. I swear!"

"Can we see his fish, Mom?" Sydney asks.

I stop the baby from eating a rock. "You did not catch a fish, Grant."

"Yes, I did!"

"No, you didn't."

"I promise I did," he says.

"And how did you do that?"

"Last time we were here, I set a trap. Now there's a fish there. You have to come see."

"There's no way. I'd have to take the kids over the stream."

"Then do it. You have to see this!"

I look him square in the eyes. "You promise you caught a fish?" I've been tricked before.

"Mom, I swear. I'll bet you a million dollars."

I exhale. "Fine." I motion Sydney over. "Hang onto my hand for as long as you can, and then you'll have to cross by yourself."

Ever the explorer, Sydney doesn't hesitate. She hangs on for a second and then leaps forward but doesn't even come close to landing on the rocks. She walks the rest of the way in the water. Her pants look worse than Grant's.

"Hurry up, Mom!" Grant calls.

I fling Ashlyn around my back. "Hang on tight to my neck," I tell her and then pick up Baby. I take my first step, landing easily on a fat river rock. Afraid to slow down for fear of loosing my balance, I keep moving. But I quickly realize my fear was irrational, for Baby has other plans. He begins to wail and thrash, determined to touch the water.

Because I'm struggling with Baby, Ashlyn looses her grip and falls into the water on her bum. I move to help her but stumble myself. By the time we're all on the other side of the stream, the only one with dry shoes is the one person who can barely walk.

"Over here, Mom!" Grant says.

I trudge up the small rise to the main section of the river.

My three older children are standing by the water's edge, staring into the water. I follow their gaze. A pale gray fish floats belly up; most of its scales are missing. Nearby is a pile of sticks roped together. *Grant's "trap."*

"Why isn't the fish moving?" Ashlyn says.

"It's sleeping," Sydney whispers.

"I caught it," Grant says.

I shift Baby to my other hip. "Nobody caught it. It just got old and died and then washed up on shore," I explain. I pick up a stick of driftwood and hand it to the Baby to play with.

"I really did catch it," Grant says.

"Uh-huh." I set Baby down. "I'll give you guys a couple of minutes to play and then we have to get back."

The kids run up and down the river bank trying to find more fish that Grant has "caught." When it's time to go, the kids do what comes natural and complain. "We're leaving!" I say and scoop up Baby, but not before removing a patch of wet moss from his mouth.

"So when are you going to pay me?" Grant says as we cross back over the stream. We don't even bother with the rocks.

"Pay you?"

"Yeah. My million dollars."

"Are you serious?"

He stops walking. "I bet you a million dollars that I caught a fish, and I did."

"You didn't catch that fish. It died."

"Because I caught it."

"You didn't catch it."

He smiles. "Prove it."

"Do you really expect me to pay you a million dollars?"

"You made the bet."

"There's no way I'm paying you a million dollars."

"Then you lied, and Dad says our family never lies."

I stop walking and turn around. "I don't lie."

He waits for an explanation.

"Double or nothing," I say.

"What does that mean?"

"It means, let's make one more bet. If I lose, I pay you two million dollars; if you lose you owe me nothing. Deal?"

He rubs the future scruff on his face. "Deal."

"I bet that I can count to one hundred before you."

He narrows his eyes. "Let's do it."

"On your mark, get set, go." I'm finished before he's even to fifty. "I win. Nobody owes anyone money."

"That's not fair!" Grant says.

"You made a deal and our family never lies. Now lets go." I start the climb back to the trail. Baby's determined to return to the water, and my left arm is beginning to burn from holding him, but I can't switch hands because my right hand is busy pulling Ashlyn up the steep embankment. She falls just as I reach the top.

"My knee!" she cries.

I bend over and brush the dirt from her leg. "It's just a little scrape. We'll put a Band-Aid on it at home." She's still crying as a place her in the carrier. Baby joins her chorus when I set him next to her. I hand him his sippy cup, which he again refuses.

I close my eyes and try to block out their sounds. *This will all be over soon*, I tell myself. I pull the bike back onto the path. Grant has replaced his tennis shoes with rollerblades. "Grant, I don't think that's a good idea. Why don't you just run home?"

"No way. I'll just hang on."

"Fine." I don't even care anymore. I just want to go home.

"Don't get too far ahead, Sydney!" I say. "Grant, can you make Baby happy?" Behind me, Grant taps on the carriage. My handlebars swerve. "Never mind. Just hold still."

I pedal hard, both to keep up with Sydney and to get home sooner. For some reason, Baby's still crying. "Why's he crying, Ashlyn?" I call back.

"Because he wants to touch the back of the tire," she says.

"He wants what?" I ask, hoping I heard wrong.

"He's trying to touch your tire," she says, louder.

I turn around just in time to see Baby's fingers reach the back tire. I slam on my brakes. Grant grunts when he crashes into the back of the carrier. I swing my leg off the bike and squat down in front of Baby. "No! No! You have to sit back," I say, but he reaches for me. "Danger!" I repeat.

"Why don't you just put the belt around him?" Grant says.

"Belt?" I look inside the cart. Hidden behind a flap of thin material I find straps. "This would've been nice to know."

"Dad uses them all the time."

"Well Dad's perfect," I mumble, feeling stupid for not even looking. I strap Baby in and continue onward.

Our home is in sight. Sydney's way ahead, pedaling furiously. We're almost there, when I hear a thump followed by a series of grunts and moans. I look behind me. Grant has fallen.

I stop the bike again, and rush back to him. "You okay?" I ask.

He's moaning and holding his knee.

"Let me see it." I move his hand away. "Nice road rash, but I think you'll live. Want me to help you up?"

He shakes his head, gritting his teeth. "I think it's broken. Call an ambulance."

"I'm not calling anyone. You're fine." I help him stand. "See? You'll be fine."

"It will heal crooked if I don't see a doctor," he insists.

"If I take you to the hospital, they'll want to give you a shot."

He looks up at me, eyes no longer brimming with tears.

"Think you can walk back?"

He nods and takes off running.

I look up ahead. Sydney's already home and waiting for us.

"Mom, Baby keeps hitting me," Ashlyn says from the carrier.

"Give him his milk," I say and hop back on the bike.

A minute later we're home, and I couldn't be more relieved. Grant and Ashlyn go straight for the TV, Baby's standing unnaturally still in the middle of the floor, and Sydney is pouring herself a glass of milk.

"What's wrong with the milk, Mom?" Sydney says. "It's coming out in clumps."

As if in slow motion, my eyes move to Baby just as he throws up. I can't say I wasn't warned.

6

Sweet Sanctuary

For the last three months, I've been reading the most amazing book. On the cover is a picture of a beautiful girl in a long black cloak, hood pulled over her head. You can tell by her expression that she's in danger, but thankfully in the distance, a stranger, presumably her hero, rides upon a horse, bareback and shirtless. And all this is happening beneath the light of a full moon.

The whole image couldn't be any more romantic, and I've been dying to finish it but rarely have time. Most days I manage to read a few pages from it in the bathroom—the one room in the house where the kids will leave me alone for more than a few minutes.

I've just set all the kids down for dinner, plates loaded. I see this as a perfect time to go and find out who the mysterious man riding bareback is. "I have to go to the bathroom," I say. "You guys eat your dinner and no fighting."

I practically skip to the bathroom, and by the time the door closes, I'm giggling. I sit down and remove the book from underneath a package of toilet paper.

Chapter 11.

Paul rode hard and fast. The beast between his legs obeyed the slightest movement of his body. No obstacle proved too difficult for the magnificent black stallion he'd purchased three years ago. For once, he was glad he'd listened to his father. If it wasn't for the speed and agility of stallion, he wouldn't have a chance of reaching Liane in time.

Already the full moon had punched a bright hole into the dark sky. It would be midnight soon, and then it would be too late. He couldn't lose Liane now, not when he'd just found her. His heart wouldn't survive. Even now he felt it thumping off beat, threatening to break.

Just up ahead, a rock wall at the base of a mountain rose sharply into the sky. To the average spectator, it would've appeared a dead end, but he knew otherwise. As a child he'd been confined within its walls, and as far as he knew, he'd been the only one to escape alive.

He dismounted his horse at the edge of the forest and crept forward, mindful of where he placed each foot. Vastire Forest was known for its hidden traps and treacherous landscape.

Although it felt like hours, in a short amount of time he reached the entrance: a narrow slit between the rocks. It looked much too narrow to allow entry to a human, but Paul knew its secret. He slid his hand across a particularly rough stone until he found a tight hole that felt as if it had been made for a man's hand. He slipped his fingers into it and pulled. A section of rock slid back no more than two feet.

Paul didn't waste time. He surged forward, spurred on by the thought of Liane in danger. He walked quickly, yet quietly, down the narrow walkway toward a soft, flickering light up ahead. He was almost there when he felt himself being jerked back.

"Where do you think you're going?" a deep voice said.

A knock at the door makes me jump. "Mom, where are the grapes?" Grant says.

"They're in the fridge."

"I already looked in there."

"They're in there, I promise."

"But where?"

"Second shelf."

"I didn't see them."

"You might have to move stuff around."

"What stuff?"

"Stuff on the second shelf. Now go! I'm sort of busy."

His footsteps fade away.

I keep reading:

Paul doesn't answer. Instead, he swung hard, focusing on a black snake tattooed across the tall man's face. He connected, but snake-face barely stumbled. Paul tried again, swinging his left, then right, fist. Both met their mark, temporarily dazing the man. For a second.

Snake-face shook his head once, as if being bothered by a gnat, then jabbed his meaty hands toward Paul's head, Fortunately, Paul was quicker. He ducked and took two steps to his left, out of reach from the slower taller man.

"We can do this the easy way or the hard way," Paul said, panting heavily.

"For you or for me?"

Paul lunged, but this time when Snake-face swung, Paul ducked and retrieved a dagger hidden within his boot. He rose and jerked forward, stabbing the dagger deep into the man's right lung. Snake-face coughed, spraying blood into the air until he fell over face first in the dirt.

"For you," Paul said and then wiped his blade. As he drew closer to the light ahead, he felt a growing heat against his skin and by the time he reached the opening, beads of sweat had broken on his brow. Very slowly he stuck his head out just enough to see what lay in the room beyond. But he was not prepared for what he saw.

A knock at the door makes me look up. I stay silent hoping the intruder will move on.

"Mom?" Ashlyn's voice says. Her voice is low to the ground, and I realize I've just made a crucial mistake.

"I know you're in there, Mom. I can see your feet."

I groan. *I always forget about the feet!* "What do you need?"

"Can I be done eating?"

"How much do you have left?"

"Some."

"How much *some*?"

I can see her shrugging through the door.

"Ashlyn, how many bites have you had?"

"Some."

"Go in there and finish eating. Seriously. This is dinner. I'm not making anything else the rest of the night."

"But I'm full!"

"Full of what? You haven't eaten!"

"But I am full!"

"Full of something," I mumble. "Now get out of here and go eat. And tell the other kids not to bother me. I'll only be a few more minutes."

She stomps away, but I don't let it faze me—my only focus is on Paul.

Except for a roaring fire on the far side of the room, the room was dark. Dancing flames turned and twisted, casting moving shadows into the heavy darkness. In one of the flickers, Paul noticed an arm dangling over the edge of what looked like an ebony casket. He moved closer and reminded himself to breathe.

Just then a folded piece of paper slides under the door. On the top it says, "Mom," and it's in Sydney's handwriting. I leave it where it lies and continue to read.

He saw her red hair first; the color of maple leaves in Autumn. It draped over her shoulders and chest as if it were holding her down inside the coffin.

"Mom? Did you get my note?"

Her eyes were closed, and he would've thought her dead if he hadn't noticed movement beneath her pale eyelids.

"Mom? I just slipped a note under the door. Did you get it?" I lift my legs and continue reading:

Paul reached for her hand and squeezed it. "Liane?"

Sydney knocks. "Are you in there, Mom?" Her fingers slide under the door, trying to reach for any part of me.

No response. Paul tried again, this time stroking her head and whispering in her ear. "I'm here, Liane. Please wake up. We need to leave this place."

Footsteps fade away. I let out my breath.

Paul leaned forward to press his lips against hers.
"You're too late," a voice said behind him.
Paul straightened and reached for the dagger he'd tucked inside his belt earlier.
"You don't want to do that," the deep voice interrupted. "Or it will mean her life. Or what's left of it." The voice chuckled.
Paul dropped the dagger and turned around slowly.

Footsteps return. A bunch of them.
"I'm telling you, she's not in there," Sydney says. "Look!"
I quickly lift my legs again.
"She is too!" Grant says. "I was talking to her like a minute ago."
I read faster.

A man dressed in a long black robe stood not far away. His face was partially concealed by a hood, but Paul recognized the deep purple scar marring his thin lips. Sinead.

Grant pounds on the door. "Mom! Come on, let us in."

"I didn't think I'd see you again," Paul said.
Sinead takes a step forward. "Nor I."

Both kids beat on the door. "Mom!"

I close the book. "What?" I snap.

"Sydney needs something," Grant says.

"What do you need, Sydney?"

"Did you get my note?" she asks.

"Yes. I got your note."

"Did you read it?"

"Reading it now." I pick it up and unfold it:

Can we make cookies for dessert? Circle Yes or No.

"Did you read it?" she asks again.

"Yes. And the answer is—"

"No! You have to *circle* the answer!"

"I don't have a pen."

"One second." Footsteps run off.

I quickly open the book.

Paul motioned his head toward Liane. "What did you do to her?"

"Only what she wanted." Sinead moved toward her, almost as if he were floating.

Instinctively, Paul stepped back. "Liane wouldn't have wanted this."

Sinead smiled and caressed her check. It took all the strength Paul had not to charge him, but he knew that would only get them both killed.

Sinead slipped his hand into Liane's and raised it to his lips. He paused, a mere inch before giving his serpent's kiss, and looked up at Paul. "Did Liane ever tell you she bore my child?"

A pen slides under the door. "Sign it, Mom!" Sydney says.

I quickly circle "Yes" and slide it back under the door. "Go finish eating," I tell her. I wait for the sound of footsteps but hear none. After several seconds, I ask, "What are you doing, Sydney?"

"Waiting for you."

"No!"

"Why?"

"Because I feel pressured, and I just want to relax."

"In the bathroom?"

I pause. "Yes. This is where I relax. Now go! And check on Baby."

"But how much longer are you going to be?"

"Not long. I'm almost done."

"Fine."

Her steps move away.

Paul was taken back, but he quickly recovered. "You lie."

Sinead lowered her hand and exposed a smile the devil would kill for. "Not about this. We were together once."

Paul shook his head, forcing the haunted image from his mind. He had to find a way to get Liane out of here! Whatever Sinead was talking about could be figured out later. Right now he just needed to focus on saving Liane. Paul brushed his hand against his thigh pocket. The silver-tipped star was still there, right where he'd put it after Lady McBride had given it to him, after insisting he'd need it.

Chubby fingers appear beneath the door. "Mama!" Baby cries. "Mama!"

"Go find Grant," I tell him.

"Mama!"

"Grant has a book. Go get it."

"Mama!" His fists pound the door. "Mama!"

"Sydney has a treat. You want a treat?"

The pounding stops.

"A cookie," I say. "Go get a cookie from Sydney."

His footsteps pitter-patter away. Too bad the poor kid doesn't realize he can't talk yet, but I guess he'll figure that out when he finds Sydney. That means he'll be back soon, and when he does he'll be mad.

Paul knew he'd only have one chance, and if he failed it could cost him his life. But his life meant nothing without Liane, he decided. While Sinead continued his monologue about his supposed relationship with Liane, Paul slid his fingers into his pocket. When he felt cold metal against his palm, he gripped the star tightly and waited.

Sinead's eyes flickered briefly to Liane; Paul took advantage of the moment. He jerked the star out fast and tossed it hard toward Sinead's chest. A millisecond before it reached the heart of the man who'd destroyed his life, a slender, familiar hand shot up and took hold of it.

A feral cry bounces off the walls of the bathroom and slides under the door along with ten little fingers. "Mama! Mama! Mamaaaaaa!" Baby screams under the door.

"Grant! Sydney!" I call. "Ashlyn!" No one can hear me over Baby. I try to keep reading.

Liane rose and stared down at the star bearing her family crest. She turned it over in her hand.

"Liane?" Paul said, visibly shaken by the sudden turn of events.

Sinead took her hand and helped her from the coffin. "I tried to tell you. Liane is not the same."

"Mama! Mama!" Hands slap at the door.

Paul shook his head. "What did you do to her?"

Sinead grinned. "Only what she wanted."

A knock at the door. "Mom, I'm done eating. Can I play Xbox?" Grant's voice says.

"Mama! Mama! Mama!"

Liane moved toward Paul. The movement was too fluid to still belong to a human.

"Liane? What did he do to you?" He tried to keep his voice steady, but even he heard it crack.

She touched his face tenderly and smiled. "You are the only human I've ever loved."

Sydney slips another note under the door then knocks. "Did you get my note, Mom?"

"Can I play Xbox?"

"Mama! Mama! Mamaaaaaaa!"

Paul searched her eyes. "I don't understand." His eyes flashed to Sinead's, hoping for an explanation.

"It means I love you." She looked back at Sinead. *"And I love him too."*

Her words are a constrictor around his heart. *"But why?"*

The door knob turns back and forth. "Mom? Can I come in? I'm bored," Ashlyn says.

"Are you going to answer my note?"

"Can I *please* play Xbox?"

"Mama! Mama! Mamaaaa!"

I keep reading. Pressure's building on all sides until I think I might have a heart attack.

"Because, my sweet Paul," Liane said. *"Sinead has given me the one thing you couldn't—a child."*

He shook his head, unable to fathom the possibility. Instead, he focused on Liane, on his love for her. "But how can you love us both?"

She looked at each of them. "Both of you have given me something I need, but now I must choose. For eternity. And I've made my decision."

Paul met her gaze and prayed his heart wouldn't break.

"I choose—"

Just then, I hear one of my children shove metal into the door knob. They're breaking in! I should've known it would come to this. Ten minutes is simply too much to ask.

I close the book gently and stroke its cover. My heart breaks instead of Paul's. It will have to wait. I open the door suddenly, and all four kids fall to the floor.

"Yeah! Mommy's out! We did it!" they cheer like bullies after a beating.

Baby throws himself into my arms. I pick him up and let the children drag me away to a fate unknown. At the last second, I turn around and glance longingly at my sweet sanctuary. "I'll be back," I whisper.

7

They Mean Well

Every Mothers Day I ask for the same thing. "Please," I beg a few days before Mother's Day, "I only want one thing."

"Anything," Grant says. The other kids nod in agreement.

"I want one day to relax. That means no breaking up fights, no cleaning dishes, no cooking, and I don't even want to see the laundry room."

"That's easy," Sydney says.

Grant smiles. "We can give you that."

"Who will cook our food?" Ashlyn asks.

Grant elbows her. "We can do it."

"Then I can't wait," I say, and I really mean it. I'm convinced this Mother's Day will be different from all the others because I couldn't have been more clear about what I wanted.

It's Mother's Day morning. I hear the garage door open at 7:00 a.m. My husband is home from working the night shift at the hospital. The back door opens, but he doesn't immediately come to our bedroom for which I'm grateful. I'm looking forward to sleeping in.

I drift back to sleep, the sounds and smells of breakfast cooking sneak into my dreams.

Twenty minutes later, my door opens and in come my husband and kids carrying a tray filled with food.

"Happy Mother's Day!" they all say.

I struggle to sit up. "Wow! What a surprise!" My body doesn't respond very well, and I slide back under the covers, only wanting to sleep.

"Sit up, Mom! I made the eggs," Grants says.

Sydney pulls the covers back; I curl up like a touched caterpillar.

Aaron sits next to me holding the tray on his lap. "If you don't get up, we'll be forced to wrestle you."

"I'm up!" I say and force myself to sit against the wooden headboard.

My husband sets the tray of food on my lap. I can barely see the stack of pancakes through a thick layer of butter and syrup—just the way I like it. My senses waken the rest of me, and I sit up straighter. "This looks delicious! Thanks, guys."

"Can you open your presents now?" Ashlyn asks.

"I have presents? I didn't ask for any."

She nods. "We got you lots of them!"

I eye Aaron suspiciously. "I can't wait."

"Let's let her eat first, guys," he says.

I nod in agreement already on my fourth bite. I've learned if I don't eat fast, the kids will think my plate is an all-you-can-eat buffet.

"Can I have some of your juice?" Sydney asks. "It's good for my skin."

I pick up the glass and drink it all gone. "What was that, Sydney?"

"Go get your own," Aaron tells her. "This is Mom's food."

Just then Baby's head appears at the top of my bed; he's climbing up and when I wonder how, I see he's thrown a grappling hook. "Where did he get that?" I ask Aaron, but he's not listening. His eyes are closed.

"Aaron?" I jiggle his leg.

He opens his eyes.

"Weren't you going to try and stay awake?" I ask, hopeful. The night before he'd promised to stay awake for Mother's Day. He'd done it before, so I hoped he'd be able to do it again.

"I'm awake," he says and straightens. "Are you almost done?"

"Just about." I stab my fork at Baby's hand, but he still manages to steal half of my pancake. "I'm done," I say.

The kids cheer. "Open my present first!" Ashlyn cries. She throws a wrapped present onto my lap, barely missing the plate of food as Aaron takes it away.

I pick up the present and shake it. "It sure is light. Is it a piece of a cloud?"

Ashlyn climbs on top of the bed to sit next to me. "How's a cloud going to help you?"

I sniff the package. "So this is something that's going to help me?"

She pokes at the present. "Just open it!"

"Okay, here I go!" I tear into it frantically.

And then I stare.

Sitting in my hands is a package of dish sponges.

"Do you like it?" Ashlyn says.

I look at Aaron who's smiling. "They're beautiful," I say. "Just what I needed."

"I thought so. I always see you doing the dishes and knew you'd love more sponges to help you."

I give her a hug. "It's perfect. Thank you, Ashlyn."

"My turn!" Sydney says and hands me a present. Baby sneaks under the blankets, and begins to crawl around.

I open Sydney's awkwardly shaped present. "Cupcake liners and spatulas?"

"Yes, so we can make cupcakes and then decorate them."

"That would be fun," I say hesitantly.

"Now mine," Grant says.

I'm afraid to open it but don't show it. Slowly I open his heavy present. "A frying pan. It's beautiful."

"I always hear you complaining about the one you have so I thought you'd like this."

"You're right, Grant. I would like this. Any mother would love to have such a fancy pan."

"I got you something too," Aaron says and sluggishly rises from the bed. "I didn't wrap it though."

"That's okay."

He moves into our walk-in closet and returns with a vacuum. "It's the nicest one on the market. This thing practically vacuums on its own."

"What does *practically* mean? Do I still have to push it?"

Aaron's fiddling with all the James Bond-looking buttons on its front. "Of course. It's not a robot."

"Does the store have any robots?" I ask.

Aaron doesn't answer because he's turning it on. "Listen

to how quiet it is? Isn't it great? Now you can vacuum while I'm sleeping."

I clench my jaw. "That's great."

He turns it off. "But that's not all we got," he says, and I perk up. "We got you flowers."

I smile. Finally a real present just for me. "Wonderful! Where are they?"

"They're in the garage," Sydney says.

"Well go get them. I want to see."

Aaron sinks back into the bed. "They're not for indoors. They have to be planted outside."

"So . . . they're like landscaping flowers? For me to plant?" *Because I love gardening.*

"Can we plant them right now?" Ashlyn asks.

"We'll do it later," Aaron says. "Let's let mom rest." He lays his head on my shoulder. The rest of the kids climb on the bed to join us, all the while trying to avoid the moving lump beneath the covers.

"So what do you want to do now?" Aaron asks through a yawn.

"Can I just rest? Watch some TV?"

"Of course."

"Can we watch the Disney channel?" Grant asks.

"No," Aaron says. "Mom gets to watch what she wants."

I turn on the television and check the DVR. I'm about to put on one of my favorite shows, when I notice Baby sneak out of the room. "Baby's getting away," I say to Aaron, but when he doesn't answer, I look down at him. He's fast asleep. I contemplate waking him but decide against it. He's worked all night, and it just didn't feel right waking him up, even if it is

Mother's Day. I can still have a good one without him, right? I know I'm lying, but I get up anyway. "Come on, guys. Let's go out and let dad sleep."

I turn off the TV and follow the kids into the kitchen where all the cupboards and drawers look like they've thrown up everything inside them. "What happened in here?" I ask, more like cry.

"What?" The kids look around.

"The mess! What happened?"

"We made breakfast," Grant says.

"For how many people?"

"Can we watch TV?" Sydney asks.

"Yes, please. All of you. And find something Baby will watch too."

Sydney takes Baby by the hand and guides him toward the living room.

As soon as the kids are settled, and I know I'll have a few minutes of peace, I look for a quiet place to rest where I won't feel pressure to clean. The kitchen's out, as is the living room, which is covered in a sea of Legos.

I walk to the dining room but find a half-completed puzzle scattered on the table.

I slip into Baby's room but find it still smells from Baby's regular morning stink pickle.

I retreat into the girls' room, but its been transformed into a stuffed animal petting zoo.

I stick my head into the office, but the work I hadn't finished from the day before stares back at me angrily.

I finally go downstairs, but when I find a fort of blankets and chairs the size of Canada, I realize there's nowhere to go. I slump down on the stairs to think. Thinking turns to anger, and anger turns to action. I stand up. "Let's clean this place," I call.

"What?" Grant says, his head appearing over the stair rail. "But it's Mother's Day!"

I march up the stairs. "And this mother can't relax in a messy house. I want this place clean in thirty minutes! I'm setting the timer."

"But I haven't eaten!" Ashlyn cries.

I deflate. "Fine. We'll eat first and then clean."

In the kitchen I look for leftover pancakes but only find the batter.

"Use my pan I got you," Grant says.

"Good idea." I cook the rest of the batter. The pan turns out to be better than all of my others, and I'm glad Grant got it for me.

"You have five minutes to eat. I'm setting the timer," I tell the kids.

"Not the timer," Grant moans.

"I hate timer days," Sydney says.

I *love* timer days. "Just eat." I set the timer and start washing the dishes. Ashlyn's new sponges come in handy.

The timer goes off. I set it again, this time for thirty minutes.

"What happens if we're not done in thirty minutes?" Grant asks.

"In bed for a long nap. All of us."

"Even you?" Ashlyn says.

"Even me." Secretly I hope they fail.

The kids work fast and fight each other hard. I'd use a timer more often as it always gets results, but it also increases the tension in our home tenfold. So I always have to decide: fast, stress-filled results, or slow, stress-free results.

The kids finish with five minutes to spare. I use this time to vacuum the family room with the new vacuum. It is much easier than my older one and seems to have been built with a seat just perfect for Baby. He rides around the room, arms outstretched. "I'm King of the World!" I imagine him thinking.

The buzzer rings. My house is clean. I collapse into the sofa and wipe the sweat from my furrowed brow.

"Can we plant your flowers now?" Ashlyn asks.

I shake my head. "Let's wait for Dad. I'm tired."

"But he's going to sleep all day! Please?"

"Mommy's tired, Ashlyn," I try to explain.

She pulls on my hand. "But we got them for you! Don't you want to see what your present's going to look like?"

"Come on, Mom. We picked them out special," Sydney adds.

I look into their eager eyes. Baby is already beating at the front door. Against my better judgment, I say, "Only on one condition. You must promise me that you'll help. I don't want to get stuck doing this by myself. Deal?"

"Of course we'll help!" Sydney says.

Ashlyn helps me up. "I can't wait!"

I take a deep breath. "All right. Let's go."

I lead them outside, and they help me gather all the tools necessary. I grab a plat of tulips and carry them to the front of the house.

"Can you dig a hole for me, Grant?"

"I will in a minute. I have to find some wood first."

"For what?"

"Be back in a sec," he calls over his shoulder and runs away.

"Sure you will." I pick up the shovel and start digging. "Sydney, can you open the bag of soil?"

"I'm not strong enough," she says while she pulls a weed twice her size.

"Fine." I set the shovel aside and rip open the bag.

"Ashlyn, do you want to help me put the flowers in the hole?"

"I will in a minute. I'm making a sand castle," she calls from the porch.

Sydney looks up. "A sand castle?"

"Do you have to do it on the porch?" I ask.

"I'll clean it up, I promise," Ashlyn says back.

Sydney runs to join her. "Keep an eye on Baby, Sydney!" Baby's playing with Ashlyn on the porch.

I dig several holes and fill them with flowers. I'm not sure if I'm doing it right, but it seems the logical thing to do. A little dirt here, add water there, and let the sun take care of the rest.

Every few minutes I call for the kids help but am always met with one excuse after another. When an hour passes and my back aches and I'm soaked with sweat, I decide I'm done, even though I've only planted half of the flowers.

I straighten and brush the dirt of my jeans. "All done, kids. Let's go inside."

"But you're not finished!" Grant calls. He's on the other side of the lawn building something with several pieces of wood.

"Yes, I am. Clean up your mess and put back that wood."

"But, Mom! I'm not done with my shanty!"

I walk over to him. "What's a shanty?"

He looks at me like I'm the dumbest person on the planet. "Serious?"

"Whatever a *shanty* is," I motion to the crudely put together pieces of wood, "I don't want it on my front lawn. Please clean it up."

"No. I want to finish it!"

"Are you really going to argue with me on Mother's Day?"

He tosses a short 2 x 4 to the ground. "This stinks!"

"It sure does." I walk off, but stop when I see a dirt city covering my front porch. "Girls, I want this cleaned up right now!"

"But we haven't finished Paris!" Ashlyn cries.

"Clean it up now or I'll go all Godzilla on it." I return to the flowerbed to put up all the tools and the rest of the flowers. It takes me several minutes, and during this time, I'm not paying attention to the kids. My only thoughts are finishing, getting back in the house, putting on a movie for the kids, and then hiding out on the toilet to read my book.

I instantly regret my neglect when I walk inside the house. There are tiny muddy footprints of what I think must be a leprechaun, visiting late, but when I follow them, I find the culprit, staring outside our front window: *Baby*. But where did the mud come from?

I open the front door only to discover that dirt Paris has now become a flood zone. Sydney stands a few feet away, in two inches of mud, holding a hose with water spraying from its spout. When she sees my expression, she takes a step back.

My voice grows louder with every word I say. "Turn the water off right now!" She dashes off to obey my command.

I look to my left. Ashlyn is sitting in the mud moving

her legs back and forth. "Leave the water on, Sydney!" I call. "Stand up, Ashlyn." She does as I ask. "You're going to hate this, but I don't care."

"Hate what?" she asks, clapping her muddy hands together.

I pick up the hose and point it directly at her.

"Aaahhgh!" she screams and tries to run away, but the porch rail stops her. I douse her with water until she's almost clean. "Okay, Sydney. Now you can turn if off."

"What a mess," Grant says from the bottom of the porch. "You guys are in so much trouble."

I spray Grant with the last trickle of water from the hose. "Have you cleaned up your mess yet?"

"No."

"Then get it done!"

He kicks at the steps and walks away. I look at Sydney. "Why did you do this?"

"I was trying to wash it off."

"Couldn't you have just swept it off?"

She looks down. "I thought it'd be easier with water."

I loosen the tension in my shoulders. "Well I guess you've learned your lesson then, haven't you?"

She nods. "How are we going to clean this up?"

"I guess let it dry and then we'll worry about it." I motion the girls inside. "Come on. Let's get you guys inside the tub."

Once the girls and Baby are settled into the bath, I clean up all the footprints, but not without glancing at the clock. It's almost three. What in the world am I going to do with the kids until bedtime?

Several minutes later, I help the kids out of the tub just

as my husband appears, eyes still tired. "I am so sorry I fell asleep," he says. "I didn't mean to."

"I know. It's okay."

"The house looks amazing. Did the kids clean for you?"

I dry off Baby's hair. "They helped me."

"You had to clean on Mother's Day?" he asks, appalled. I'm glad to see someone else thinks that's a crime.

"And we planted flowers!" Ashlyn tells him as she climbs out of the tub.

"Did you guys plant them or did Mom?"

"Mom did," Sydney says from behind him. "And she did a great job."

Aaron looks at me, eyes sad. "I am so sorry."

"It's fine. Just another day."

He shakes his head. "No. It's not." He leaves the bathroom with us following behind. "I'm taking the kids," he says.

"Forever?"

"For a few hours. We'll go to the park or something."

I stop him. "You mean you're going to leave me here alone in the house?"

"Is that a problem?"

My brain has stopped working. "I don't get it."

"What don't you get?"

"What will I do?"

"Whatever you want."

The possibilities race through my fogged brain. "I'll be in my house with no kids," I whisper.

"You okay?" he asks.

My eyes meet his. "When are you leaving?"

"As soon as possible." He turns to the rest of the house and yells. "Get dressed, kids! We're going to the park!"

Cheers bounce off the walls. Faster than they've moved all day, they are dressed and waiting by the back door. I'm still standing in the middle of the floor.

"Say good-bye to your mother," Aaron tells the kids.

"Smell you later!" Grant says.

"You can borrow my nail polish if you want," Sydney calls over her shoulder.

"Don't play with my dinosaurs!" Ashlyn adds.

Aaron gives me a kiss on the cheek. "Have fun doing whatever you want," he says.

Whatever I want? I hear the door close. Then . . . nothing. The sound is new and foreign. The sound is so sweet, a single tear escapes from a buried emotional reservoir.

Very slowly I move forward, afraid to disrupt the silence. *Whatever I want.* I don't stop moving until I'm in front of the stereo in the living room. I open the CD drawer and reach to the very, dusty back and pull out the first thing I touch. Music begins to play, bringing memories back from the days I was carefree. In a complete daze, I turn up the volume. Sounds that don't involve singing vegetables or rapping dinosaurs flow into me, igniting me with new life.

I undo the button of my pants and unzip. My jeans fall off me like old skin. In one swoop my shirt comes over my head, and in a move my husband would kill to see, I snake the bra out from under my tank top and fling it across the room. It lands in the garbage.

Finally free, I jump on the couch in time with the beat of the music. My hips begin to move and arms wave in some ancient primal dance. I'm in this current trance, when I hear a throat being cleared.

I freeze and slowly turn to the back door. There stands my husband and all four kids. Poor Baby looks like he's going to cry.

"We forgot jackets. It's chilly outside," my husband says, trying not to laugh. "Kids, go back to the car. I'll get your stuff.

I step off the couch with the grace of Elizabeth Taylor, attempt to pull my tank top down over my underwear, and pick up my jeans. "I'm doing laundry," I say.

When the kids don't move, Aaron says, "Go!" They bump into each other as they try to escape the frightening scene before them.

"Reverting back to your old ways so soon?" Aaron says as he opens the front closet.

I turn off the music. "I don't know what you are talking about."

"Uh-huh. Well have fun doing whatever you were doing. I won't keep you anymore," he says and walks out with his arms full of coats.

As soon as the door closes, I run to the front window and wait until I see the car pull out of the driveway, and then I wait some more. When I feel confident they aren't returning any time soon, I take my party to a more private setting: my bathroom.

Moments later, I'm soaking in the tub with my favorite book in one hand and a Fat Boy in the other. Despite how the day had started, I truly feel like a Queen. And that makes for the best Mother's Day ever.

8

A Plague Be upon My House

T he day starts out as any other, but there are subtle signs that tell me things are about to get worse. At first I think nothing of the fact that my oldest son doesn't want to eat.

"I'm not hungry," he says and nothing more. No obnoxious comment. No complaining. Instead of wondering why, I revel in his silence. He sits on the couch next to his sisters watching TV, not even bothering to fight back when their feet clearly cross over "the line."

Meanwhile, I'm getting Baby and myself ready for a family party. We're supposed to leave in twenty minutes, and for a change, we're right on time. The girls have been bathed and dressed, Grant's ready, and the Baby has already pooped, so I'm thinking this is going to be an easy trip.

When it's time to leave, all the kids pile in the car except for Grant. I find him still sitting on the couch, motionless. "What's going on?" I ask him.

He shrugs. "I don't know."

"Do you feel okay?"

"My stomach hurts a little."

"Hmmmm. You think you'll be okay to go to the party?" I'm really hoping he says yes, because I've had this party planned for a couple of weeks now, and I'm in charge of dessert. "Your cousins are all going to be there. We'll be playing games. And there's treats." Right when those words leave my mouth I know I have him, but at the same time, I have a sneaking feeling that I've just cursed myself.

"I guess I can go." He stands and slowly makes his way to the car.

"That's the spirit," I say. "You'll be having so much fun that you won't even think about your stomach."

Grant doesn't respond. He simply climbs into the front seat of the car.

"Everyone's seat belts on?" I ask and start the engine.

I get a yes from everyone but Baby, who's only word is still "Mama."

The drive to the party is about twenty-five minutes by freeway. The kids have all brought books to keep them occupied. "We'll be there soon," I say as I merge into 75-mph traffic. I settle into my seat, cruise control set, music playing low onto the station I like and not my husband's. I'm feeling good, relaxed even. Baby has fallen asleep (praise the heavens), and I find myself daydreaming—a luxury I don't often get.

I'm in this current state of bliss when my dream is shattered by the most horrible sound coming from my son. It starts low in his throat and then comes loud and fast out his mouth like a cement truck dumping the last of its load. The sound is accompanied by a dark brown liquid pouring from his throat. And a lot of it.

It happens so suddenly that I can only stare. And drive. One great big barf. All over his pants.

I'm about to ask if he's okay, when the gut-wrenching sound comes again. The truck has more to dump. More puke to deliver. This is when I start screaming for the girls to hand me something, anything, because by the looks of it, it ain't stopping.

Within seconds there's a jacket in my hands. I don't have time to ask if there's anything better; I simply shove it into my sons lap to catch the last of his "everything-must-go sale." When he's finished, Grant's face is whiter than my sun-deprived legs, and he's holding his arms out, looking at the slimy vomit dripping from his skin. "Mom?"

"It's okay. We'll be there soon." *In twenty minutes.* Just the look and moldy smell of him makes my tummy have woes of its own. "Sydney, hand me the baby's wipes, please," I ask. A second later, I'm handing Grant wipes one by one so he can clean himself off.

"It's all over me, Mom. What am I going to do?" he asks.

That's what I'm wondering too, but I don't tell him that. "We'll figure it out." Just then I think of my sister who lives close to where the party is. I quickly dial her number. "Do you mind if we stop by for a few minutes before the party?"

"Sure."

"And can you have a few items ready right when I get there?"

Like what?

"A pair of gloves, garbage bag, rags, the strongest cleaner you've got, and a change of clothes for Grant."

She wants to know what's going on, but I can sum the story

up into two words: car vomit. No other words are needed. She has four older kids and has been through it all.

The drive to her house is unbearable. Both girls are crying because of the smell, Grant's crying because he doesn't feel well, and I'm crying because that's all I seem to do anymore.

But at least Baby's sleeping. I try to focus on that.

When I arrive at my sister's house, she's standing in the driveway ready for battle. I help ease Grant from the passenger seat, only to find it's worse than I feared. Throw up has breached the pant barrier and penetrated into the seat. Not just a little bit either. There's a cesspool foaming where my son's bum once sat.

"Wow. You're going to need a lot more cleaner," my sister says. "I'll bring some out after I get Grant in the shower."

Much to Grant's embarrassment, we insist he strip down before he enters her house. He's reluctant at first, but when we tell him he can either stay in his clothes the rest of the day, or strip right now, he opts for exposure. Once his wet, stinky clothes are off, and he's standing on the lawn in just his underwear, we finally let him go into the house to shower.

Meanwhile I'm left with the task of cleaning out the car. I know every second is precious as I'm sure the barf is burrowing deeper and deeper into the cloth upholstery, but all I can do is shake my head. I have no idea how to get rid of it. When a vomit bubble pops, I'm spurred into action. I tear off a handful of paper towels and absorb as much as I can. The towels are soaked immediately. I repeat the process again and again until no more standing liquid remains.

Now comes the tough part.

I take more towels and press them into the seat. After just

a few seconds it's soaked. I close my eyes and clench my jaw, completely frustrated.

"Here. Try this," my sister says from behind me.

"A window squeegee?"

"Yeah. They work wonders in cases like these."

I doubt it, but I take the squeegee anyway. I start by pressing it deep into the back of the seat and pull forward. Hidden bile rises to the surface and drips to the floor as I swipe it across the seat. To my chagrin, I have to repeat this motion several more times.

There have been times in my life when I've wished to be somewhere else, but I've never wished to *be* someone else. Angelina Jolie would be nice, but right now I'd settle for my hoarder neighbor who has more rabbits than square footage.

"That's the most disgusting thing I've ever seen," my sister says from behind me. "Do it again."

I scrape the seat, pressing harder. Still more bile. Over and over it returns like a Yellowstone Park stink pot. "I can't keep doing this," I say. "The party starts in five minutes."

"Just get what you can," my sister says. "I'll go check on Grant."

I pick up a bottle of cleaner. With so little time, I decide to do the most logical thing (at the moment it seemed logical). I remove the cap and pour the entire bottle on the seat. And soak up the excess with rags. To ensure the seat has been totally disinfected, I repeat the process with two more bottles.

My sister returns with the rest of my children and a pale-looking Grant. "Maybe you should just go home," she says. "I can take care of the party."

"Does your stomach still hurt, Grant?" I ask.

He nods.

I inhale deeply. "All right," I exhale. "Let's get you home."

"But what about us?" Sydney says. "I have party hair."

"We'll have a party at home," I say, trying hard to hide my own disappointment. I open the back of the SUV and give my sister the cupcakes I had painstakingly decorated hours earlier. "Here. Make sure people savor each and every one of them."

She swaps me the cupcakes for several freezer bags— emergency barf containers. "Will do. Hope you feel better, Grant."

"Thanks again," I say and begin to load up the kids, but this proves difficult. The car smells like a dead cow that's been marinating in formaldehyde. Even Baby fights being strapped into his seat.

I don't answer my children's pleas for mercy, and I ignore their tears. *If you think being a bystander to sickness is rough, just wait and then you'll really be hating life*, I want to tell them. I know it's just a matter of days before they become afflicted with the same illness as Grant. I look in the rearview mirror and see both girls and the Baby with their fingers in their mouths.

Make that hours.

On the drive back, I call and cancel every appointment, every meeting, and any social event I have planned for the next week.

"How come?" a friend asks.

"CDC is shutting us down. We're quarantined for the next while."

"Good luck," she says. I can hear the sympathy in her

voice. She's a mother too and understands the hell I'm about to go through.

We make it home without another incident. I tell the girls to watch the Baby while I take care of Grant. I move to help him into his room, but he stops me. "Can I lay in your bed," he asks.

"No, you need to be in your own."

His eyes and shoulders sag. "But you're too far away. Please? I want to be close to you."

My hardness crumbles. How can I say no to that? Against my better judgment, I lay him down in my bed. On my pillow. I pretend I don't see the diseased air puff from his mouth and attach itself to my pillowcase. "You okay?" I ask after I've stripped him down to his underwear to help him cool down.

Grant nods and closes his eyes. I let him sleep.

An hour later I hear him calling for me. "Mom! I need a barf bucket! Quick"

I race to the kitchen and grab the nearest bowl. I make it to him just in time before he blows grits. His spine arches up until I think it might pop from his skin. And the way his jaw appears to unhinge makes me wonder if he's turning into a werewolf. I'd laugh if he didn't look so miserable.

"Can I have a drink?" Grant asks, after wiping his mouth.

"Sure. I'll bring you some water." I leave carrying his barf bucket. Holding my breath and turning my face away, I dump his stomach sewage into the toilet.

Grant's back asleep when I bring him his water. I really do feel bad for him. For a few moments, I stroke his hair, but the tender moment doesn't last. Ashlyn appears at my bedroom door holding her stomach.

"My tummy hurts, Mommy," she says.

"Do you feel like you're going to throw up?"

She nods.

"Let's set you up on the couch."

"Noooooo!" she wails. "I want to sleep in your bed!"

I tighten my lips, but say, "Okay, but you have to be quiet. Grant's sleeping."

"Can I watch TV?"

"If you keep it down." I lift her into the bed and cover her up. "You feel warm. Do you want something to drink?"

"Yes."

"K, one second."

I get her a drink and her own barf bucket. It's just a matter of time.

The next few days move slowly. Grant gets better, and Ashlyn's over the worst of it, but now both Sydney and Baby have it. I've flushed so much goulash gush that I'm afraid I've plugged up the city's water treatment plant.

I'm holding Sydney's hair back while she spews into my fancy glass bowl (I haven't had time to wash the others), when my husband comes home from work. "You're home early," I say. It's only eight o'clock at night.

"I don't feel good," he says and collapses into our bed next to Sydney.

"Are you going to need a bucket too? Cause I think I'm out."

He grunts.

Not sure what that means, but I'm hoping it means he can

make it to the toilet. Kid puke is one thing, but adult barf? He's on his own.

After I dump the contents of Sydney's emptied stomach, I tuck her into bed and then turn my attention to my husband. I untie his shoes, cover him up, place a glass of water and a bucket next to him and then kiss him on the forehead. Then I leave to check on Baby, who's lying lethargic in Grant's arms.

Baby's warm but not as hot as he was a few hours ago. I take him from Grant and rock him in the same recliner that's served as my bed the last two nights.

I'm so tired I can barely keep my eyes open, but I push through it. What else can I do? I'm Mommy; there's no one else.

Two more days pass and finally everyone is well. My husband stayed in bed an extra day just to make sure. Personally, I think he loved the attention, especially the predator call I gave him to blow (his idea, not mine) whenever he needed something.

It's almost midnight. I've stayed up late to clean and disinfect my home. It still stinks, but with time the smell will fade. All the kids are in bed, and my husband is fast asleep. Because he missed the last two nights of work, the hospital has asked him to pick up a few day shifts starting in the morning. I let him rest even though I'm starting to feel achy. I ignore it and crawl into bed.

Not more than twenty minutes later, I'm dashing for the bathroom. I throw up several times, emptying my stomach along with what feels and looks like my intestines. My body shakes and sweat pours from my head. Because I'm too exhausted to stand, I lie down on the cold tiled floor, chills bursting across my skin like a lightning storm.

The house is quiet. Even the air seems to rest, ever so still.

No one is aware of my suffering. It's only me, the porcelain bowl, and the cold floor. Because I can't sleep, I begin to sing:

"Nobody knows the troubles I've seen;
Nobody knows my sorrow.
Nobody knows the trouble I've seen;
Glory Hallelujah!
Sometimes I'm up, sometimes I'm down;
Oh, yes, Lord.
Sometimes I'm almost to the ground."

I lie there for several hours until I can finally drag myself to the bed, only to return to the bowl again for another quick drop-off.

Finally, I'm back in bed and almost asleep when my husband's alarm goes off at 5:30 a.m. I don't say anything as he gets ready. There's nothing to say. He has to work, and I have to be Mom. He goes into the bathroom and then comes back out.

"Why does the toilet look like a bomb went off in it?"

"I'm sick," I say.

He comes over to me and feels my head. "You going to be okay?"

How do I answer that? "Eventually."

"If I could call in sick, I would, but I already missed too many days."

"I know."

"Hang in there, okay? Love you," He pats my back and leaves for work.

I want to beg him to stay, but I don't. Instead I try to catch some sleep between severe stomach cramps.

By seven o'clock the kids are awake. It's time to get them

ready for school, but I can't bear the thought of getting out of bed.

Sydney sticks her head into my room. "Mom? Are you getting up?"

"In a minute."

"I need you to sign my homework."

"I know."

"And I need a cold lunch."

"I know."

"And can you tell Grant to be nice? He called me a lush."

"You're not a lush, sweetie."

"Will you tell him that?"

"Yes."

She pauses. "Right now?"

I count to ten. "In a minute. I'm not feeling well."

She closes the door.

Very slowly I sit up, my head spinning. I will myself to stand, bend over and wait for a cramp to pass, and then make my way into the kitchen.

Grant's poured himself a bowl of cold cereal. Next to him, the sugar container is empty. "How much sugar did you use?"

"Not much."

"Uh-huh." I get a bowl and spoon for Sydney and hand it to her. My body aches so much I imagine myself peeling the skin from my bones just so I can massage the soreness from them.

"Aren't you going to talk to Grant?" Sydney asks.

Leaning against the counter, I look at him. "Don't call your sister a lush."

"She doesn't even know what that is!" he says.

"Neither do you." My stomach rolls, overtaking my intestines with it.

"I do too!" Grant says, Rice Krispies spraying from his mouth.

I don't argue; I'm running for the nearest bathroom instead.

"What's wrong?" Grant calls.

I sit on the toilet, my stomach exploding out my backside. The chills and sweat start all over again, but what really has me worried is a familiar tightening in my throat. "Sydney!" I yell. "Bring me something quick! I'm going to throw up!" I hear a scurrying of feet, crashing of dishes, and fighting voices. "Hurry!" I say.

Sydney comes running into the bathroom holding a shallow, rectangular cookie sheet.

I shake my head, tears welling in my eyes. "This isn't going to—" But it's too late. I snatch the pan and let the brown cow out. Vomit splatters back into my face.

When I'm finished, I'm wasted. I slump into the back of the toilet seat, balancing the full sheet cake on my lap. I have to wait several minutes before I have enough energy to finally move.

It's then I employ my split personality, someone named Fragancia (I stole the name off the tampon box next to my toilet). I let Fragancia figure out how to deal with the sheet cake of barf while getting off the toilet. I also let her deal with the rest of the day: getting kids dressed, breakfast, and driving them to school. Fragancia is super mom, and I let her do all the work until Baby takes his nap, giving me time to rest.

When the afternoon comes and my strength returns, I wonder how I managed. I had no one to cook my meals, help me get dressed, or hold my hair back while I downloaded dinner. I was alone and yet I managed. And I know I'm not the only one. Mothers all over the world have to do what I just did. I wonder for the millionth time why mothers are not ruling the world. It's basically doing the same things we accomplish everyday—cleaning house, laundry, budgeting, multi-task-ing—just on a much larger scale.

I throw open the windows and let the cool, fresh air rush in, destroying any remnants of the toxic bug. I take a shower, shake off the last of my illness, and wait patiently at the door. When my husband comes home from work, I give him a quick kiss on the cheek and say good-bye.

"Where you going?" he asks.

"Movie and dinner."

"By yourself?"

"Yup."

"Are you feeling better?"

"Good enough. Dinner is in the oven."

He stares after me, still confused. "Are you having an affair?" he calls after me.

I turn around and smile. "Not anymore. John and I split ways this morning."

9

Sports Spectacle

Like every other parent, I want my children to be well rounded. I want to expose them to all sorts of new experiences until they find one that "fits." So far our family has turned out to be very physical and competitive. Maybe this has something to do with our nightly wrestling matches or diaper throwing contests. Whatever it may be, my children love to compete.

For this reason, I've signed Grant and Sydney up for basketball. It seemed the logical thing to do. Little did I know how much more stress it would add to my life.

It's Saturday morning. Both Grant and Sydney have basketball games. Sydney's starts at 10:00 a.m. and Grant's is at 11:00. That means we're going to have to book it between games, and already I'm dreading the transition.

"Are you guys getting dressed?" I call to the girls, while scrambling eggs on the kitchen stove. "Breakfast's almost ready."

Sydney walks out from her room. "I can't find my jersey."

"Did you look in the laundry room?"

She sighs and walks by me. "Not yet."

"You need to hurry. We leave in twenty minutes and you still need to eat."

Sydney throws her arms to the ground. Luckily they're attached to her body so they do nothing but make a slapping sound on her thighs.

"Watch it," I warn and turn off the burner. I lean over the stair rail to call down to Grant. "Come and eat, Grant!"

Before I return to the kitchen, I peek in on Aaron who's getting Baby ready. "How's it going?"

"Good, if I could get this kid to hold still." He's holding Baby down, trying to change him, but Baby keeps rolling over.

"You need to use your whole forearm to pin his chest down while your free hand changes him."

"Nah, he'll listen to me," he says while dragging Baby back toward him. "Hold still, Baby. I command it!"

"Good luck, then," I say and walk off.

Sydney meets me half way into the kitchen. "I still can't find it," she says.

I shake my head. "It's got to be here. I remember washing it from last week and that was on Monday so it's got to be in your drawers."

"Well it's not."

I glance at the clock. "Just go eat. Eggs are on the stove. I'll look for your jersey." I turn around and go into her room where I discover Ashlyn still in her pajamas. "Get dressed! We're leaving in fifteen minutes!"

"I don't want to go," she whines.

"Too bad. Now hurry up or you're not going to have time for breakfast." I walk into her closet. "By the way, have you seen Sydney's jersey?"

"No."

I open Sydney's drawers and search them thoroughly. No jersey. I look under her dresser and to the sides. When I can't find it I slump against her wall, thinking. I *know* I washed it.

I walk back into Baby's room just in time to see Aaron finishing up changing the Baby; his forearm is pressed against Baby's chest. "So you thought you'd try it my way, eh?"

"This isn't your way. See how my arm is slightly tilted?"

"Uh-huh. Right." I walk into Baby's closet and look inside his dresser. "Hey, have you seen Sydney's jersey?"

"Are you serious? Don't we have to leave soon?"

"Yeah. She can't find it."

Aaron stands up, holding Baby. "Grant, Sydney, and Ashlyn! Stop whatever you're doing and come here!" As if he's waved a magic wand, they suddenly appear in front of him. "I want all of you to look for Sydney's jersey. Grant, I want you to look in your drawers. Ashlyn, you look under beds. Sydney, you look everywhere else. Go!"

They scatter.

"Why can't they keep things where they belong?" he asks me.

"That's like asking me, 'What is the secret to the universe?'" Aaron and Baby follow me into the kitchen. "You want some breakfast?"

"Is there time?"

"If you hurry. See if you can get Baby to eat something too. I'm going to go search the laundry room again."

A few minutes later, the kids return. Sydney is crying. "We can't find it anywhere!"

"I found these," Grant says. He's holding two old jerseys.

I take hold of the smaller one. "Will this work?" I ask Sydney.

"It's the wrong color!" A tear slips over her red cheek.

I hold up the other jersey. "What about this one?"

"It's too big!"

"Just wear it, Sydney," Aaron says, after shoving cereal into his mouth. "We're out of time."

"But it's not my number!"

I kneel down in front of her. "Nobody looks at the numbers. It's not a big deal. Now lift your arms." I'm trying to keep my voice calm because I sense a major breakdown coming. For both of us.

"But you don't understand!" she says, her voice rising. "I have to wear *my* jersey. The coach said. What if I have the same number as someone else?"

"What do they do with those numbers?" I ask.

She thinks, then throws up her arms. Again, I'm grateful they're attached. "I don't know, but I have to have my own!"

"They don't do anything with them," Grant says as he's tying his shoes. "Quit being such a baby."

"Stop it, Grant!" I say.

Sydney cries even harder.

"If you can't calm down, then we're just going to stay here," Aaron tells her. "You can't go to a game crying."

I wave my hand, trying to silence him. As a girl, I recognize the signs of a female meltdown, and any comment from a guy right now, even if it's a nice one, will come across all wrong and only escalate the problem.

I look at Sydney and say in a very soft and gentle voice. "I understand you're frustrated, but I promise you, no one will notice that this number is not yours. Now please raise your arms. You're going to do great today."

She's not happy but lifts her arms anyway. I pull the jersey over her head—definitely too big. More tears burst from her eyes. "It looks like a nightgown!" she says.

Behind me, I sense Aaron opening his mouth. I glance over my shoulder and silence him with a look. "This can be fixed," I say. "Don't worry. Come with me." I take her hand and guide her into my bathroom. "The rest of you make sure you're ready!" I call.

I open the designated hair bow drawer in my bathroom and remove a rubber band. "The other day on TV," I say to Sydney who's wiping at her eyes, "I saw the cutest girl with pig tails. She was wearing a red skirt and a long white shirt." While I'm talking, I'm bunching up the bottom of the jersey into a sort of ponytail on her side. "On the bottom of her shirt she had made this really cute bow. Sort of like this." I step away from her so she can look down and see what I've done. "Do you like it?"

She tilts her head. "Maybe."

"I think it's cute." I stand and bow to her, my hand extended. "Shall we get going, my lady?"

She giggles and gives me her hand. Together we walk into the kitchen, but her smile disappears when Grant begins to laugh. "Your shirt looks so dumb!" he says.

Sydney's emotional volcano erupts; tears stored in a deep reservoir burst from her face.

I storm over to Grant, wanting so badly to tackle him to the ground and put him in a headlock, but Aaron steps between us.

"I'll deal with this, you deal with that," he says and motions his head toward a hysterical Sydney. My eyes stay locked with Grant's.

"Go," Aaron says. He physically makes me turn around.

Knowing nothing will make Sydney feel better until she's emotionally drained, I simply pick her up and let her cry on my shoulder. "Ashlyn!" I call.

She appears in the hall. "What?"

"Will you grab the diaper bag? We're leaving."

Her eyes grow big. "But I haven't eaten!"

"Too bad. I told you to eat a while ago."

"Huh? No way! I'm starving!"

I rub Sydney's trembling back. "Why weren't you hungry five minutes ago?"

She shrugs.

I let out a long, loud sigh. "If you hurry, you can get a sandwich bag of cold cereal, but get the diaper bag first."

She dashes toward Baby's room. Sydney's still crying on my shoulder, but I feel her body begin to relax, and I know soon I'll be able to talk to her.

"Are we about ready?" I ask the boys.

Aaron finishes his lecture to Grant who looks like he's going to cry too. Aaron straightens, picking up Baby with him. "Let's get in the car."

Ashlyn comes running into the kitchen. "But I haven't gotten my cereal yet!"

I take the diaper bag from her with my free hand. "Then hurry!" I set Sydney down. "Go get in the car, and while you're in there, I want you to think about what you want for Christmas."

This gets her attention, and she looks up at me. Her normally blue-green eyes are a watery aqua color made even more vibrant by her red puffy eyes. "When is Christmas?"

"In like three months, but I need to start planning now. Do you think you can come up with some ideas?"

She nods, and a smile cracks like the first rays of a glorious sunrise.

"That was pretty good," Aaron says, after Sydney leaves.

I walk by him. "I wasn't handed the 'Mom' title for nothing."

"Where's Ashlyn?" I ask when I'm almost to the car.

"She must still be inside," Aaron says.

I turn around and walk back into the house. "Ashlyn?"

"Just a second!" she calls from the pantry.

I walk over and open the door. Ashlyn's stuffing a handful of cereal into a sandwich bag—from off the floor. The whole box of Captain Crunch has spilled everywhere. "What happened?" I cried.

She blinks and swallows. "Sorry, Mom."

I don't have time for this. "Just get in the car. Go now."

She hurries off with me on her heels.

Inside the car, I turn around from the front passenger seat and ask Sydney, "So did you decide what you want for Christmas?" The puffiness in her eyes is slowly fading, and a smile has replaced her frown.

She rambles off a long list, and soon the whole car is buzzing about Christmas—the last thing I want to think about, but at least it's made Sydney happy.

We pull up to the red-brick middle school where Sydney will be playing her game. Her team is already there and practicing. "Hurry out there," I say, after removing her jacket. "You're going to do great!"

"Good job making her happy," Aaron says when we sit down. "I didn't think it was possible."

"Girls just need a soft voice and an understanding ear."

"More like Midol and a box of chocolates."

The game buzzer sounds, bleeping out the curse word directed at my husband.

Sydney walks on to the court with four other teammates. She glances around sporting a huge smile; her whole body is tensed and ready to play. This is her third basketball game, so I'm hoping this time she'll get to handle the ball. In every other game she simply runs up and down the court really fast. In fact, I don't think she's figured out that there's even a ball in the game yet. One day she'll get smacked in the head with it and wonder, "Where did that come from?" Maybe that day will be today, I hope.

After the tip off, Sydney takes off running. Every time she's the first to the basket, but as soon as the rest of her team catches up, she sprints to the other basket. Because of the high turnovers that often occur in little kid's basketball games, most people don't realize what she's doing. But I do. She thinks she's racing.

Sydney runs by and gives me the thumbs up.

"What is she doing?" Aaron asks.

"She's winning."

"Huh? She's all the way down there while her team is over here."

I just smile and continue to watch. That is until Baby decides to bolt from Grant and run onto the court. I leap to my feet to grab him, but it's too late. A first grader has just plowed into him. The ref blows the whistle and scowls at us. I quickly pick up my crying baby and rush him off the court.

"Sorry," I mouth to everyone around us. Only the mothers give me understanding, sympathetic looks. The men simply snarl at me for interrupting the game.

"Why aren't you watching your kid?" Aaron mocks when I sit down.

"Shut it," I growl and hand him Baby.

The game doesn't last long. Sydney didn't touch the ball again, but she sure ran fast. "We won!" Sydney cries when she sees us.

Aaron gives her a hug. "Good job, Sydney. You ran really fast."

She beams.

Sydney's teammate appears next to her, grinning and looking at me expectantly. And then another one shows up. I smile back at them. "Good job, guys," I say, but when another player appears, I glance at Sydney nervously. "Do your friends need something?"

"They're waiting for treats," she says.

"Treats?"

"Yeah, you brought treats for us didn't you?"

Aaron looks at me. "Were we in charge of treats?"

Blood drains from my face.

"What did your mom bring us?" A girl with pigtails asks Sydney.

Sydney shrugs. "What did you bring, Mom?"

My mind's blank, but then I remember. I unzip the diaper bag and peer inside. Besides the smashed graham crackers in the bottom, it looks there's only one thing that might soothe the bellies of hungry six-year-olds—a box of baby rice cookies. I pull it out of the bag and smooth a big dent in its side.

"What are those?" Sydney asks.

"They're rice crispy treats. For winners," I say and give each kid a few of them.

A boy with a head like a basketball sniffs one. "They smell like carrots."

"That's the smell of winners!" I say, then lean over to Aaron and whisper, "Let's get out of here quick!"

He doesn't argue, but when we get inside the car, he starts laughing. "That was awesome! Nice job forgetting the treats."

I want to laugh with him; I see the humor in the situation, but it also reminds me of how inadequate I feel. As a mother, I often see more wrong with myself than right. It didn't used to be that way, but now that I'm torn in so many directions, I can't remember which way is up half the time.

Aaron glances over at me. "Did I make you feel bad?"

I stare out the window. "No. Just mad at myself."

"It's no big deal. The kids got a treat. It's not like there's rules on what you're supposed to bring. Don't worry about it."

I know he's right, but still.

"So are we going to my game now?" Grant asks from the back seat.

"Yup. Your game starts in ten minutes," Aaron tells him.

We drive across town to a different school. The parking lot is packed with minivans and SUVs, all waiting expectantly for their owners. Cheers and the rhythmic thumping sound of a basketball against a polished court drift out the open gym courts making us move faster.

"Can I play after the game?" Grant asks from behind me.

"No. You have chores to do," I say as I'm getting Baby out of his car seat.

"But I haven't played with anyone forever!"

"You had a friend over two days ago." I walk away before he can harass me further.

"Here, let me take Baby," Aaron says.

I hand him over. "Thanks."

The gym is as crowded as the parking lot. The game before ours has three minutes left on the clock. We stand on the sidelines and wait for a seat to open up. Grant maneuvers his way next to me. "Mom, can I please play?"

"Grant, I already told you no."

"But that's dumb! Why can't I play?"

I speak through my teeth. "I don't need to give you a reason. Besides, I already gave you one."

"But cleaning? Really? I can do that anytime."

"Then why didn't you do it yesterday when I asked?"

He exhales big enough that I smell his breath.

"Go stand next to your father," I say and nudge him away.

He doesn't go. Instead, he folds his arms tight and scowls. "This is so dumb. I don't even know why I'm here. I hate basketball."

I turn to him, appalled. "Are you kidding me? You are the one who begged me to sign you up!"

Still scowling.

I get Aaron's attention. "Can you talk to Grant please? He's having some issues."

Aaron turns to Grant. "What's going on?"

"I just want to play with my friends after the game."

"What did your mother say?"

Grant looks at me, more like glares. "No."

"Then there's your answer. Why are you arguing?"

He shakes his head. "This is so dumb."

I cringe inside, knowing that was the wrong answer.

"Come on, Grant," Aaron says, taking him by the arm. "Me and you need to have a talk outside."

At the same time they leave, the game ends. I move to the bleachers and find a seat. Grant's teammates run onto the court and begin to practice. A few bleachers up, Ashlyn and Sydney run back and forth. Baby's on my lap playing with my cell phone. I wait a few minutes then decide to go see where Aaron and Grant are. "Girls, I'll be right back."

I stand up carrying Baby and walk outside. Grant is leaning against the brick wall of the school looking madder than ever. "What's going on?" I ask.

Aaron looks at Grant and waits a moment before answering. Finally, he says, "We're leaving. Let's go, Grant."

"What!" Grant cries.

"Get in the car, now."

Grant's eyes widen. "Are you kidding me?"

"Now!" Aaron storms off. Grant bursts into tears and follows after him.

"A little clarification?" I call after him, but he doesn't turn around. I'm left standing in the doorway wondering what I'm supposed to do. Is Aaron simply taking him to the car for a long time out, or did he mean we're all leaving?

I turn back around and go inside, thinking I'll wait to see if Grant comes back. The game buzzer sounds and Grant's team begins playing. I try to pay attention, but my eyes keep looking to the doors. After several minutes of fighting to keep Baby on my lap, I begin to feel stupid watching a game my son isn't even in. I turn around. "Let's go, girls," I say.

"What? Why?" Sydney asks.

"I'll tell you outside. Come on." I stand up and step down the bleachers.

Outside, Sydney asks again, "Why are we leaving?"

"Because Grant's not playing anymore."

"Why?"

"Because he got in trouble." The car's just up ahead; smoke billows angrily from its tail pipe.

"What did he do?" Ashlyn says.

"Probably mouthed off." I open the door to the backseat and buckle Baby in. "Hop in, girls."

Once they're all in, I open the passenger door and climb in. Behind me, Grant's crying. "So I guess we're leaving?" I say.

Aaron's stares straight ahead but says, "What part of 'we're leaving' did you not understand?"

"What part of 'a little clarification' didn't you understand? Don't get snappy with me!"

He relaxes into his seat. "Sorry."

"What happened?" I ask.

Aaron looks in his rearview mirror at Grant. "Grant had major attitude and he couldn't turn it around. I gave him three chances, but he still wanted to go head-to-head. I feel bad he had to miss his game, but he's got to understand that he can't act like that." He looks in his rearview mirror again. "Right, Grant?"

Grant nods, arms folded tight.

Aaron pulls the car onto the road.

At first I'm annoyed that Aaron kept him from playing,

but after a few minutes of thinking about it, I realize that's the best punishment he could've done. Playing sports is not the most important thing in life. It's about helping children to become good, well-rounded individuals who can function in society, even though they may not always get their way. By letting him play, we would've been telling him that his attitude was acceptable.

I turn around in my seat and look at all my children. It's been a crazy morning, no different than any of the others, but my role as a parent has been solidified. It's not about making sure my children have the right kind of clothing or have the best treats to give out. It's not even about making my kids the star players. It's about teaching them life lessons. You win some and you lose some. And although Grant may think he's lost today, I know he's won.

10

Case of the Missing Christmas Spirit

The Christmas season arrives, striking fear into my heart. I dread it every year: the constant begging with every commercial the kids see, the swarms of shoppers trying to get the nicest toys at the cheapest prices, the overspending, the constant Christmas music everywhere I go. You name it. You might say I'm a bit of a Scrooge.

But this year I want to change.

I want to feel the Christmas spirit that my grandfather spoke about when Christmas meant an orange and a candy stick, carols for neighbors, and family gatherings. Those were the good ol' days, and it's something I want to recreate for my own kids. "I want" will be a thing of the past.

And so I swear by the stars in the skies that we're going to feel the Christmas spirit, even if it kills us.

To help my kids get in the mood, I bring my Christmas tree out early. It's one I'd purchased at a charity event a few years ago, and it's beautiful. But that's not why I love it. The decorations are wired on, including a four-foot antiqued Santa shoved deep into its branches. Setup is a breeze.

When we're finished, we decorate the rest of the house with what few Christmas decorations I own. In my storage closet, I have ten storage bins. Two are reserved for Christmas, and the rest are for Halloween. Maybe that's the problem.

"Where'd all our decorations go?" Sydney asks.

I look from a tattered angel to a scuffed-up nutcracker. We do seem to be missing some. "Let's go look in the utility room. Maybe they're in there."

The kids follow me downstairs, singing what words they know of "Jingle Bells." I open the utility room door and flip on the light.

"This place is creepy," Ashlyn says.

"It's not bad. We just don't go in here that much. See what you can find, kids." The place is filled with camping gear, ten-year-old food storage, broken furniture just waiting to be fixed, and unmarked boxes. Tucked in the farthest corner of the room, I find our old Christmas tree. We decorate it every year and keep it downstairs, but because the kids always end up fighting, I'd be happy if we never set it up again.

I step in front of it, hoping the kids won't see it. I want to get the Christmas spirit, not to destroy it. The kid's eyes seem to pass over the worn box. Relief pours into me, and I follow the kids out of the room. Just as I'm about to shut off the light, Grant says, "What's that?"

"What?"

I follow the direction of his pointed finger, burrowing into the box.

"We haven't looked in there," he says.

"Sure we did, remember?"

"No we didn't. One sec." Grant dashes to the back of the

room. I'm half tempted to turn the light off and lock him in here, but before I can properly formulate my plan, Grant says, "It's our old tree! Can we decorate it? Please?"

"It's our tree?" Sydney cries.

"What tree?" Ashlyn says.

"Please, Mom? Can we decorate it?" Grant asks again.

Maybe this time will be different, I tell myself. "Fine. Bring it out."

Grant and Sydney slide the box on the floor, knocking over several items in its way. "Oops," they say when something heavy crashes.

I don't even want to know. "Just keep coming," I encourage.

They drag the box to the side of our family room. "Right here?" Grant says.

I open the box. "Perfect." Tucked on top of the tree branches are the rest of our decorations. I pull them out first and then ask for Grant's help to remove the three sections of the tree. "It's in pieces, so be careful. Find the bottom first," I say.

"Is this it?" Grant asks, holding up what looks like a green pipe with spiky needles sticking out.

I look it over. "I think so. Hold it down, and I'll put in the middle piece."

In no time at all, our tree is complete.

"What's wrong with it?" Ashlyn asks.

"It's sad," I say.

She touches its fake branches tenderly. "How come?"

"We need to decorate it, and then it will be happy," I explain.

"I don't think decorations will help it," Grant says. "I think they're broken."

I don't want to admit he's right. The branches clearly have issues, but I don't want to draw attention to that fact. "Come on, guys! Let's make this tree pretty!"

The kids take up the task. The first few minutes are really enjoyable, and I don't regret taking it out. Everyone's getting along and helping each other, but the moment is ruined when Baby discovers that a long string of red beads makes for a great weapon. He whips them over his head, yelling loudly, and then let's them fly. The front end hits Sydney in the face and the back end whips Ashlyn's neck. Both girls turn and look at each other. Thinking the other is the cause, they attack each other, tears stinging their eyes.

Grant, who saw the whole thing, grabs Baby and pushes him to the ground. "No, no!" Baby joins the girls in their watery parade.

I take hold of Grant. "What are you thinking? I'm the parent around here." I straighten. "Aargh! Can't I have one Christmas without fighting?" They stare at me wide-eyed. "Can't I?" When they don't answer me, I add, "Maybe we should just cancel Christmas."

Now Grant cries.

I sigh and close my eyes. Four kids crying, three broken tree pipes, two girls fighting, and a partially decorated house. *Merry Christmas.* Before I cry too, I storm up the stairs and sit on a chair alone. I hear the kids. Two are still crying, while another two argue. Something has got to change, and I resolve right then and there that the change has to begin with me.

I stand up and inhale deeply. "Everybody upstairs!" I call.

A herd of elephants answer the call. I ignore the sounds of shoving and fighting as they make their way to me.

"Yeah, Mom?" Grant asks.

I wait for Baby to join the pack, before I say. "We are going to make treats for the neighbors. Who'd like to help?"

They all raise their hands.

"But what about the tree?" Sydney asks.

"We'll finish it later after we've made treats and after we've watched *A Christmas Carol*. Are you guys ready to have fun?"

They cheer.

"Good! Come on, let's get started."

And so operation "Christmas Spirit" begins.

We make treats for the neighbors. I ignore the spilled chocolate chips on the floor (Baby will eventually find and eat them all). We deliver gifts. I ignore the fighting when they argue over who gets to ring the doorbells. We watch *A Christmas Carol*. I ignore the kids when they say:

"When is someone going to pull out a sweet karate move?"

"Is there a dinosaur in this?"

"If they're poor, why doesn't Bob move his family to a different city and get a better job?"

"Why doesn't Scrooge just take a sleeping pill?"

I ignore it all and force a smile; any moment now Christmas spirit will pour into me.

It's Christmas Eve, and the kids are acting like they've downed a keg of maple syrup. They are literally bouncing off the walls. Baby has two bruises on his head to prove it.

"You guys have *got* to settle down!" I say while I place the candy trains we've just made out of Baby's reach.

Ashlyn's jumping on the couch. "How's Santa going to come to our house? We don't have a chimney."

"I'll leave the front door unlocked. Get off the couch."

She jumps down. "Can I sleep by the door?"

"No."

Ashlyn's running in circles. Sydney and Grant chase after her. "How is Santa going to fit a dinosaur into our house?" she asks.

I remove Baby from off the table. "He's not bringing you a real dinosaur."

Ashlyn stops suddenly. Grant and Sydney collide into the back of her. Normally this would make her cry, but I can tell she's only thinking about one thing. "But I asked Santa for a dinosaur," she says.

I take away a pair of scissors from Baby who's trying to cut the cord to the TV. "And maybe you'll get one, but it won't be real."

"Dinosaurs don't exist anymore," Grant says.

Ashlyn frowns. "But Santa said he'd bring me one."

"Which Santa?" I ask.

"The only one there is," she says, innocence bleeding from her eyes.

"I mean, when did Santa say this?" I clarify.

"At the hospital."

I think. "At daddy's work party?"

She nods.

Grant laughs. "That wasn't the real Santa!"

"Was too!" Ashlyn says.

I step in between them and call, "Aaron!"

He's wrapping presents in our bedroom, but after a few seconds, he sticks his head out. "Yes?

"When do you think we can put the kids to bed?"

"Are they ready now?"

"No!" All kids yell. Baby falls to the ground crying.

I think fast. "How about if I let you guys sleep by the tree downstairs?"

They huddle together to discuss their options. Baby stands in the middle, staring up at them, no doubt wishing he could voice his opinion.

When a minute passes and still no answer, I'm afraid of what I might do if they say no. I think of the Nyquil in the back of the medicine cabinet.

Grant steps away from the pack. "We'll sleep downstairs," he says.

I exhale. "Awesome. Go get your sleeping bags while I put Baby to bed." Baby falls to the ground crying again.

An hour later, the kids are where they should be, but their mouths are more active than ever. But I don't mind. They are singing Christmas songs, even though they don't know most of the words. Aaron and I are upstairs quietly laughing at their creative renditions:

"Deck the halls with brows of Molly, fa la la la la la la la!
Tis the reason to be crawly, fa la la la la la la la la!"

I notice the time. "We should probably put the stockings and the rest of the presents out. It's getting late."

"What about the kids?"

I consider sharing my Nyquil idea with him. Instead, I say, "I'll go put some sleepy music on, and you fill the stockings."

"On three?" Aaron says, his hand outstretched.

I place mine over his. Together we mouth, "One, Two, Three!" then split ways, working quickly so we can move on to our most favorite Christmas tradition. Just us. Alone in our room.

I go to sleep peacefully.

At 2:00 a.m., my eyes open. I see only darkness, but feel the presence of somebody lingering at the foot of my bed. It hovers close, willing me to give it a sign that I am awake. I turn over.

"Mom? You awake?" Grant asks.

"Yes, but why are you?"

"Is it time to get up?"

"For what?"

"Christmas."

"What time is it, Grant?"

He pauses. "One."

"Not time yet. Go back to sleep and don't you dare wake the other kids."

"Can I just peek in the living room?"

"Not if you want to keep your eyes. Good night, Grant."

"'Night," he mumbles and leaves the room.

I sit up and listen closely to make sure I hear his footsteps go down the stairs. I do and collapse back into bed, falling instantly asleep.

I dream I'm shopping in Wal-Mart on Christmas Eve. It's crowded, and I'm trying to avoid the hordes of people wheeling their full carts past me. All of them seem to be heading to the same place as me—the Baby aisle. But I need diapers. *Desperately.* I've already circled the aisle three times, but the crowd swells, fighting me back. Finally, I decide to charge right in, but the wheel of the cart suddenly snags on something, stopping my momentum. I push harder.

"Mom," I hear one of the other shoppers say.

I tilt the cart up, trying to free it.

"Mom!" This time the voice is that of a child's.

I let go of the cart and look around.

"Mom!"

Just then a woman three times my size bounds down the aisle pushing a cart full of dog food. It's a heavy load and it's picking up speed. I try to escape, but I'm blocked on all sides. My gaze meets that of the hefty dog-food wielding woman; she has no intention of stopping. Just before she crashes into me, I hear, "Mom!"

My eyelids fly open, and I gasp for breath.

"Mom?"

"Sydney?"

"I can't sleep. Is it time to get up?" Sydney asks. I can barely see her darkened silhouette.

I wipe sweat from my brow and glance at the clock. 2:18 a.m. "Not even close. Go back to bed."

"Can I clean my room?"

"Nice try. Go back to bed please."

"Fine." Her footsteps fade away.

I drift back to sleep.

This time I'm in the kitchen. Alone. Forty people are coming over in ten minutes and dinner isn't ready. The buzzer on the oven goes off. I open it and am accosted by billowing smoke. My roast is ruined. *Burned.* What am I going to do now? The kitchen is a mess, kids are fighting, dinner isn't ready, and when I look down, I discover I'm naked. But to top it off, I realize my kitchen is on the edge of a cliff. I stumble back, frightened, but end up slipping on spilled milk. I burst into tears just as I slide off the cliff.

I sit up, gasping for air. There's a figure at the foot of my bed. Before it can speak, I say, "Go to bed! It's not time.

When you see light outside, then you can wake me up. Go! Be gone!"

The figure sniffs and walks away. I collapse back into bed. Three a.m. Because the panic of my last dream still lingers, I'm awake until four. Finally I sleep.

Someone is shaking my shoulder. "Wake up! It's Christmas!"

It's Aaron's voice.

"What time is it?" I ask.

"Six."

"Are the kids awake?"

"I don't think so. Let's go wake them."

"No! Please let me sleep." I tuck the covers around my chin.

He shakes me again. "Come on. Let's get up. I can't sleep."

This time I cover my head. "Watch TV or something."

Grant sticks his head in the door. "I heard voices. Are you guys up?"

"No," I snap, but Aaron says, "We are. Go wake the other kids."

When Grant leaves, Aaron jumps on the bed, on top of me. "Aren't you excited? It's Christmas!"

I moan and try to turn over.

Aaron hops off the bed and throws back the covers. "Do you want to see a sweet wrestling move I just learned?"

I sit up. "I'm up. I'm up."

The kids come running into our room. Grant carries Baby.

"Can we go see what Santa brought?" Ashlyn asks.

Aaron blocks the door. "Before we go, I want to remind you all what Christmas is about. Can anyone tell me?"

"It's about the birth of Jesus," Grant says.

"And that giving is more important than getting," Sydney adds.

"Do you think I got a dinosaur?" Ashlyn asks.

Aaron ignores her. "You're right, kids. Christmas isn't about getting presents. It's about remembering Jesus and all that He did for us. Okay?"

They nod, smiling ear to ear.

"Family hug and then you can all go," he says. The hug lasts milliseconds before they tear off into the living room. Aaron takes my hand and follows after.

The kids dive into their stockings first, practically disappearing inside them. "Slow down," I say. "We have all day."

But they can't hear me. The ripping sounds of candy wrappers and the tinkling of trinkets drown out my voice, but I don't mind. The kids are happy, and I'm happy.

In addition to a few smaller presents, each kid receives one big present from Santa. Grant gets a bow and arrows, Sydney gets a stuffed bear that she can feed, Ashlyn gets a big bin of dinosaurs, and Baby gets to play with all the boxes and papers unsupervised. All of them are happy. I'm grateful that we were able to give them a good Christmas when I know there are others who aren't so fortunate. I only wish my kids can understand how blessed they are.

It's then that I begin to formulate my plan. I don't even tell Aaron about it. I wait until all presents are opened, and the living room is a sea of boxes and wrapping paper before I make my move. I stand up suddenly. "My phone's ringing. I'll be back, but while I'm gone, why don't you guys clean up?"

They don't move until Aaron says, "You heard your mother. Clean."

They spring into action just as I disappear into my room to "answer" my cell phone. I wait three minutes and then return. "Family meeting," I say.

Aaron gives me a "what's up?" look, but I just shake my head. "Come on kids, sit down. I have to tell you something. Grant, grab Baby." The girls hop on the couch, but Grant is a minute longer as he's trying to pull an ornament out of Baby's mouth. When they finally sit down, I say, "I just got off the phone with someone very important."

"Who?" Sydney asks.

"Was it Santa?" Ashlyn says.

I look at each of them with my most serious expression. Even Aaron looks worried. "It was the mayor of Blackfoot."

"What's a mayor?" Ashlyn says.

"He's the man who makes sure all of the people in Blackfoot are taken care of."

"Why did he call you?" Sydney asks.

"He needs our help."

Grant looks skeptical. "How does the mayor even know who you are?"

"Serious? You may not know this, Grant, but I'm quite popular around town." I look at Aaron who's rolling his eyes. "Right, Dad?"

The kids all look to him for confirmation.

"Oh sure. She's quite the celebrity," he says in all seriousness.

"Anyway," I say. "The mayor called because he needs our help."

Sydney leans forward. "With what?"

"There are some families with kids your same ages who didn't get anything for Christmas."

Ashlyn frowns. "Why wouldn't Santa give them anything?"

I pause. I hadn't thought this far into my plan.

Aaron jumps in. "Because Santa couldn't find their houses, and he ran out of time. It happens sometimes, unfortunately."

"That's sad," Ashlyn says.

"It is sad. That's why the mayor called. He's wondering if we can give away some of our toys to the kids who didn't get anything."

Their silence sucks cold air into the room.

"Say what?" Grant says.

I shift in my seat. "The kids who don't have anything are the same ages as you guys. That's why the mayor called."

"Well I'm not giving my bow!" Grant says.

"And I don't have any toys to give," Ashlyn says right after him.

"You have a ton of toys, Ashlyn." I inhale deeply and blow it out. "Come on, guys. Think about this for a minute. There are kids out there just like you who have nothing. Look around! You guys have everything. Surely you can share. Remember what Christmas is all about?"

The chill in the room warms slightly. Sydney jumps up and disappears into her room. Grant slowly follows. Ashlyn remains seated.

"Ashlyn, don't you have some toys you can give?" I ask.

She shakes her head. "I've got nothing."

I lean forward. "So you're telling me that if I walk into your room, I won't find any toys?"

"Not any I can give."

I tighten my lips. I know she's four, but I don't think I'm asking anything too difficult of her. I try again. "There is a little girl, your age, who has no toys. Will you please go into your room and find something nice for her? Please?"

She moans, but gets up. As soon as she leaves, Aaron whispers, "Did the mayor really call?"

I laugh. "Do you even know who the mayor is? I sure don't."

"Then what are you doing?"

"Just a little social experiment. I want to see what our kids will do."

Aaron turns sideways on the couch and props his feet up. "This ought to be good." Baby sits next to him with a sucker in his mouth.

Grant returns first, holding a new DVD that Sydney had given to him. Because I was with her when she bought it, I know it came from the dollar store and is of some cartoon he's never heard of, or anyone else for that matter. "Is this all?" I ask.

His mouth drops open. "What? This was one of my presents."

"Come on, Grant. Surely you have something nicer than this. Get back in your room."

He clenches his fists and opens his mouth to argue, but a click of a tongue from his father sends him away.

Sydney returns next carrying a necklace that I gave her. "This is good, Sydney. Go put it on the table." She walks over and sets it down. I know she liked the necklace, but I think she can give more. "Do you also have a toy you can give?"

"I'll go check." She crosses paths with a very unhappy-looking Ashlyn.

"What do you have, Ash?" I say.

She hands me her old Dora backpack with a broken handle. "Really? A broken toy? Why don't you get one of your dinosaurs?"

She gasps like I've just slapped her. "I can't do that!"

"Why?"

She thinks really hard before answering. "Because the other little girl doesn't like dinosaurs."

"How do you know?"

"Because I know!"

"Ashlyn," Aaron says sternly. "Go get one of your toys. A nice one this time."

She throws up her hands and storms off. "I guess I'll just give all my toys away!" she shouts.

"That will work too," I call after.

Grant's back. He's holding a remote control helicopter. He didn't get it for Christmas, but I know it's one of his favorites. "Do you think the boy will like this?"

I lift my eyebrows. "You really want to give this?"

He shrugs. "Sure. I bet the kid will love it."

"I bet he will. Good job, Grant." I give him a hug. "Go place it on the table."

Baby, who's been watching closely, seems to catch on to the "game." He jumps from the couch and starts picking up whatever he can find on the floor and places it on the table.

Sydney appears. "Will this work?"

I look at what she's holding. "You tell me, Sydney. If you were this girl would you like to open a present and see a naked Barbie Doll with messy hair?"

She shakes her head, but her feet remain planted.

"So what are you going to do about it?" Aaron says.

She looks over at him, eyes sad. "Find a better one."

"Good," he says.

Sydney walks away, but I stop her. "Sydney, this is about making another girl like you happy. You don't need to be sad about it."

She nods her head and returns to her room.

"So how's your experiment turning out?" Aaron says, smiling.

"Disappointing."

"What did you expect?"

I lean back. "I expected them not to think of themselves and bring me their nicest Christmas presents."

"Really?"

"Yes. Is that so unrealistic?"

He nods. "What have our kids ever done for other people? Have they served others less fortunate? Do they know what it's like to go without? To have nothing? Face it, our kids are spoiled."

"So how do we change that?"

Aaron sits up. "We need to find opportunities for them to serve."

I think about it.

Sydney and Ashlyn return together. Sydney's holding a fluffy brown teddy bear—one of her favorites, and Ashlyn is giving away one of her new dinosaur puzzles. But they look miserable.

"Much better, girls. Go put your stuff on the table," I say.

Sydney walks away, but Ashlyn remains, staring down at the puzzle.

"Can you go put it with the rest of the stuff?" I ask.

She shakes her head.

"Can you hand it to me then?"

She moves the puzzle toward me, but when I try to take it, her hand snaps back.

"I'm not going to wrestle it from you," I say.

She tries again. When the puzzle is in front of me, I try to take it, but her death grip won't let me. "Remember the girl? You're going to make her so happy with this."

She lets go. "Can I see her?"

When I don't answer, Aaron does, but I'm not listening because I'm stuck on Ashlyn's question. *Of course!* My experiment is faulty. I'm asking my children to give to a faceless stranger, and I realize they're too young, at least Sydney and Ashlyn, to understand how their good deed could help another person.

While Aaron talks to Ashlyn, I bound up the stairs to my office and Google "poverty." It doesn't take me long to find a picture of two young girls huddled together against the side of a brick wall. They appear cold and hungry, and the camera has caught the sadness in their eyes. I quickly print it, then return.

"I just checked my emails, and the mayor sent me a picture of two of the girls," I say and sit down.

"Let me see it," Grant says.

"In a minute. This is for the girls. Come here Ashlyn and Sydney."

When they are standing in front of me, I hand the picture to them. I watch their faces as they study the two girls. Their eyebrows draw together, and when Ashlyn touches the face of the youngest looking girl, she bites her bottom lip.

"What are their names?" Sydney asks.

I think fast. "Beth and Amy."

"I know a Beth," Sydney says quietly.

"Where's their Mommy?" Ashlyn says.

"I don't know."

Sydney's face brightens. "I know something she'll like!" She runs off.

Ashlyn still holds the picture. "I think she will like dinosaurs," she says.

"Really?"

"Yeah. See the dirt right here?" Ashlyn points to the ground the girls are sitting on.

"Yes."

"She'll want to play dinosaurs in it."

"I bet you're right."

Ashlyn takes a deep breath then walks to her room carrying the picture.

"Wow," Aaron says. "Way to manipulate them."

"What? Was that wrong? They needed to see faces."

"Actually it was pretty smart."

"What are you guys talking about?" Grant asks.

"Nothing," I say.

A few minutes later the girls come back pushing a laundry basket. It's full of toys and clothes. I even see a few dinosaurs sticking out.

"You want to give all that?" I say.

They nod, but most important, I see that they are smiling. My heart melts. For once I feel like my seemingly never-ending life lessons have worked.

"Good job, girls. I am so proud of you!" I give them each a big hug. "These girls are going to be so happy when they see what they get for Christmas."

"You guys are awesome," Aaron says. "How about we watch one of our new movies while mom gets this stuff ready to deliver."

"Can we watch Jurassic Park?" Ashlyn asks, happy as can be.

"We'll see. Go downstairs and turn on the TV. We'll be down in a minute."

The kids race down the stairs with Baby sliding down after them.

Aaron and I walk to the table to examine the items. In addition to the toys and clothes the kids have given, there's my shoes, a sippy cup, a frying pan, a wad of toilet paper and a toilet brush. I sigh and smile, not even caring that Baby was obviously in the bathroom unsupervised (I'll wash his hands later).

Aaron places his arm around me. "Good job. I think you taught them something."

I shake my head. "I didn't think that was possible."

"So what are you going to do with all this stuff?"

I shrug. "I hadn't got that far."

"Might as well give it away. Salvation Army or something."

I agree. Aaron gives me a hug then disappears downstairs, but I stay to look over the items one last time, smiling. It's in this moment that I finally feel the Christmas spirit, and I know my kids have felt it too. I was so busy trying to think of how to make us all feel it, that I'd completely missed the point—that Christmas is about love. The love Christ Himself gave to all of us. And when we feel love, we want to share it with others.

I turn around, fully possessed by the Christmas spirit, and walk downstairs to join my family.

11

Blink. Blink.

It's that time of day on the specific time of the week when I'm wet, angry, stressed, and exhausted all at the same time. "Time for a bath," I yell, my voice traveling to every nook and cranny of the house. Like cowboys to a dinner bell, the kids come running. I don't know if I should consider myself lucky or not, but my children love bath time. It's me that hates it.

I send the girls to one tub and the boys to another. Because of Baby, I help the boys first, making sure the temperature is just right. Grant steps into the bath water, but Baby dives in head first—the first of many splashes.

The girl's manage to run their own bath, but it's not long before the fighting begins.

"Mom!" Ashlyn yells.

I hurry down the hall and into their bathroom. "What's going on?"

"Sydney won't play with me," Ashlyn says.

"It's not play time, it's bath time," I say as I kick their dirty clothes against the tub to catch any spills. "No fighting or you'll have to get out right now. Do you guys understand?"

"But, Mom, can't Sydney let me have the cup?"

"Share. Both of you. I mean it. You have five minutes."

"Ten," Sydney calls after me.

I return to Grant and the baby. "How's he doing?" I ask Grant.

"Good, but he's splashing like crazy."

Baby sits near the faucet, repeatedly clapping his hands into the stream of water pouring from the faucet.

I sit on the toilet and put a towel over my lap. "No, no, Baby. Be good."

He stands up and then falls back into the water, laughing. I smile despite the water spraying over the tub's edge. "Make sure you wash his hair, okay Grant?"

"I will."

"Mom!" Sydney yells again.

"Mom!" Ashlyn calls.

I place the towel against the tub and walk back to the girl's bathroom. "What?"

"Ashlyn hit me."

"Sydney hit me."

"Good. It sounds like you both deserved it. Time to get out."

"Nooooo!" they wail and hug each other tightly. Enemies then friends faster than you can say "headache." I cave. "Fine, but only a few more minutes. Wash your hair, okay?"

"But we don't have any shampoo," Sydney says.

"I'll get some in a second." On my way out of the bedroom, I notice their dirty laundry pile is starting to resemble a person; I think I even see it wave. Afraid a strike of lightning might bring it to life, I quickly gather as much as I can and carry it to the laundry room. I start a load and then return to the boys and a tub full of bubbles. "All done with the shampoo?"

Grant beams an angelic expression, and says, "What shampoo?" But I see the devil in his eyes.

"The shampoo. I need it now."

"Don't the girls have their own?"

"Come on, Grant. Where is it?"

He traces his fingers through the bubbles. "It's gone."

"Gone? It was a brand new bottle." Baby disappears beneath foaming clouds. When he pops back up he looks like a lamb. "Please tell me you didn't use all the shampoo for bubbles."

"It was him," Grant says, pointing at Baby.

Baby takes hold of his finger and twists until Grant cries out and jerks it away.

"Tell me what happened," I say, staring at Grant.

He shakes his head as if he's afraid Baby will hurt him again for ratting him out.

"Start talking or I'll ground you from the computer."

Grant's eyes shift from mine to Baby's. I give my best impression of Al Capone, hoping he'll fear me more.

It works.

Grant's confession spills from his mouth like bad milk. "Baby grabbed the shampoo and started drinking it, so I knocked it from his hands and it fell into the water. But then Baby took it again and started spraying me with it and it got in my eyes. I tried to stop him, but then I couldn't see, and I couldn't get the soap out of my eyes because Baby was smacking the shampoo bottle over my head. When I could finally see again, the bottle was empty." He looks at me, pleading. "It wasn't my fault! I promise!" He blinks. Twice.

I crouch next to the tub. "I have two questions, Grant."

He swallows. "Yeah, Mom?"

"First, how did Baby open the bottle, and second, how did shampoo get on the ceiling?"

His gaze moves to the ceiling and then returns to mine.

Blink.

Blink.

Swallow.

Blink.

His finger rises from the bubbles, like a ghost from a grave accusing their murderer. "Baby!"

"Are you seriously going to tell me that this little baby—" I look over at Baby who's smiling and sitting quietly—"managed to screw the top off the bottle and whip it hard enough that it made it all the way to the ceiling?"

"Yes." A drop of pink shampoo drips from the ceiling to Grant's head.

"So this whole thing," I wave my arms around the room, "is Baby's fault, and you played no role it?"

He shakes his head.

And blinks.

I straighten. "Fine, but you better clean this mess up when you get out."

He doesn't argue with me, which means he played a part in it just as much as Baby.

I walk across the house to my bathroom and retrieve the fancy shampoo—shampoo that wasn't on sale. I hand it to

Ashlyn. Sydney's under the water holding her breath. "Don't waste this, please. It's mine."

"Okay, Mom."

Sydney sits up. "Can you get us some more toys?" she asks.

"Are you kidding me? You guys can barely move," I say, eyeing the mound of "things" swimming with them. I think I spot a TV remote but it disappears between a dinosaur and a measuring cup. "No more toys."

"Mom!" Grant calls.

"What?" I shout. My tone's becoming more shrill and loud, but I can't help it. It seems every time I hear the word "Mom," a layer of nurturing peels back, exposing a raw, emotionless, cave-like woman.

"We have a problem! Come quick!" Grant yells.

I bolt. The girls jump out of the tub and follow behind me.

"What's wrong?" I ask Grant. He's sitting on the edge of the tub. Baby's in the middle eating bubbles.

Grant points at something floating in the corner. "What's that?"

"Move over," I say and lean in to inspect.

My heart sinks and tears come to my eyes. I look at Baby. "Why?"

"What's wrong, Mom?" Grant asks.

Very calmly, I say, "Move out of the tub, Grant, and wrap a towel around you. You're going to use the girls' bathwater when they're finished."

"What's going on?" Sydney asks. Both girls are standing in the doorway naked, water dripping all over the carpet.

I want to scream.

I want to freak out.

So I do.

"Get back into the tub right now! Aaarghhh!"

The girls dash off like fired bullets from a gun. I hear what sounds like a tidal wave when they jump back into their water.

Closing my eyes, I count to ten. I'm only to three, when Grant asks, "What's in the tub, Mom?"

I take Grant by the arms and hiss in his face. "My worst fear. I thought I'd never see it again, but there it is. It must be a boy thing. Why, Grant? Why?"

"What are you talking about?"

I let him go. "Poo, Grant. Poo."

It takes a minute for him to realize what I'm saying, and when he does, he freaks out more than I had. "Poo! You mean I've been pooed?"

I nod my head.

Grant bolts for the girl's bathroom, but I stop him. "You can't go in there!"

He hops on each foot. "Well I can't just stand here with poo on me!"

"You'll have to wait until the girls are done."

He tightens the towel around him. "No way. No way!"

"Just don't think about it." I turn toward the girls' bathroom, "Hurry up, girls!" I yell.

Grant notices a package of wipes on the floor. He removes one after another and scrubs his body until I think his skin might fall off. I should stop him, but Baby's caught my attention. The bubbles have fizzled out, leaving me a clear view of the damage.

It's bad.

I react quickly, reaching my hand into the water and pulling the plug. At this point I'm not sure what to do. It's been so long since this has happened that I can't remember how to deal with it.

I finally decide to let the water drain and then give Baby another bath but soon realize that's a dumb idea. Already the drain is getting plugged, and Baby's beginning to play with his own poo boats.

"I've got an idea," I say to Grant who's using the last of the wipes on his face. "Do you want to take a shower in my room with Baby?"

One eye twitches. "Is he going to go in there too?"

"No, he's finished."

"He better be."

"Go get it started, and I'll bring Baby in a sec."

Grant runs off, his towel a flapping cape.

Back in the tub, the water slowly drains. Poor Baby sits in the middle, looking like a brown spotted calf. I remove a towel from under the bathroom sink and say, "Stand up, little smelly one. Mommy's going to clean you up."

Baby stands, and I wrap the towel around him. "Up we go." I carry him into my bathroom and open the shower door. "Watch him close, Grant. Just let him play on the floor."

He takes Baby. "Fine, but if he poops again, I'm out of here."

"Deal." I close the door and return to the bathroom, but not before stopping in the kitchen to grab a plastic knife.

Back in the bathroom, there's barely any water in the tub, but what's left isn't going anywhere. I take the knife and begin to stab at the sewage clogging the drain. This helps a little but not much. I was hoping it wouldn't come to this, but I then wonder why I hope for anything at all.

Removing toilet paper from its holder, I wrap a bunch of it around my hand and then begin to wipe at the tub. This method proves most effective. Several more wads and toilet flushes later, my tub is functioning again.

"Looks good, Mom," Sydney says from behind me. Her pajamas are on.

"Thank you for getting your pj's on without me having to ask. I love that," I say.

Sydney smiles.

"Why don't you get something to drink, and then you can watch TV for ten minutes before you go to bed."

"Awesome!" She gives me a hug.

"Get your sister too."

"K, Mom." She dashes off.

When I'm finished cleaning the bathroom, I find the kids, except for Baby, sitting on the couch watching TV. Baby's crawling on all fours and sliding his head on the carpet. Naked.

"Couldn't you have gotten him dressed, Grant?" I ask.

Grant's not listening.

I sigh and walk to Baby's room for a diaper and pajama's. After I get him dressed, I say, "It's time for bed, guys, and I don't want any arguing."

They argue a little, and finally, after I threaten a lecture from their dad, they do as I ask.

Once I have them all snug in their beds, glasses of water on their head boards, stories in their brains, and kisses on their cheeks, I make the rounds, picking up shoes, coats, backpacks, and pretty much everything else the kids own. I end up in the girls' bathroom. The tub is still filled with water and in its center is my expensive shampoo, the lid open.

I bend over and pick it up. It's much too light to be my nice shampoo anymore. I tip it upside down; water pours from its top.

It's me who stares now.

Blink.

Blink.

12

A Day at the Beach

T he kids are bored. How do I know this? How do I *not* know this? They've only told me a thousand times in the last hour. School ended and summer break began—two days ago. And apparently it's my responsibility to find something for them to do. At least that's what they keep telling me.

It's only ten in the morning, and I'm already thinking about bedtime. I've already colored with them, played Mother May I and Hide-N-Seek, cleaned, mowed the lawn, and watched TV. I could put in a movie and let them zombie it up, but it's only the second day of summer. I save my TV parenting for the end of summer when I've got nothing left to give.

My wheels turn, as rusty as they are, and I come up with a plan. It's risky, but I think it will work.

Far away from the kids, I call one of my friends who also has four kids similar ages to mine. "Are you going as crazy as I am?" I ask Lynn when she answers.

"Completely. What am I going to do with them all

summer?" she says, and I recognize the tone of her voice. She's close to breaking.

I cover my hand over the phone's receiver and whisper, "I know this might sound crazy, but I was thinking—"

"Yes?"

"What about the beach?"

She pauses. "The beach?"

"Yeah. I heard they've cleaned it up." Next to our small town, there's a lake. Not a huge one but big enough for boating, and on its south shore there's a sandy beach. "It could be fun."

"The kids would love it," she agreed.

"We could use it as a reward to get our kids to clean."

"Deal. What time?"

"Two o'clock?"

"Perfect. I'll meet you there."

I hang up the phone and call all the kids into the living room. They come running in, anxious to have something to do. Baby toddles behind them and then climbs on my lap. "I am going to be going somewhere totally cool, and I want you guys to go with me."

"Really?" Sydney says.

"Where?" Grant asks.

"Can I ask a question?" Ashlyn says.

"In a minute," I say. I make eye contact with each of them. "If, and I mean *if*, you get your work done, then I will take you to the beach with Lynn's kids."

Grant stands up. "The big lake? Really?"

I nod.

"Where's the beach?" Ashlyn asks.

Sydney turns to her. "You know that great big lake kind of by the airport?"

"I think so."

"Mom's going to take us swimming there."

"Not only swimming," I say, "But you can each take a cup to try and catch minnows."

"What are minnows?" Ashlyn asks.

"Really small fish," Grant says. "So we're seriously going to go?"

"If you get your work done."

"What do we have to do?" Sydney asks.

I hand them each a list and they scurry away. For the next hours my house hums with production. There's no whining. No complaining. No fighting. I'm in heaven.

But then they're done.

I've already packed the car: beach towels, folding chairs, blanket, lunch, sun block, diaper bag, and more towels. I am prepared. Nothing can go wrong when you're prepared.

The kids pile into the car, and we're off. The lake is only eight minutes from our house; the kids count each one out loud. I practically kick them out of the car when I finally park.

It's a beautiful day. The sun's shining and there's not a cloud in sight. A slight breeze makes the heat more bearable. I inhale deeply as my kids roll in the sand. The air smells good—not the typical smell of potatoes burning from a nearby potato factory. Two boats are in the water, kicking up the perfect size waves for the kids, and we're the only people on the beach. Just right.

Lynn's not there yet, so I choose the best spot I can find beneath the only tree on the beach. Its four meager branches provide little shade, but I don't complain. I could use some sun. Last night my husband asked if I'd been putting teeth whitening gel on my legs.

I lay down a blanket. "Take your clothes off here, and then you can go into the water—after you put on sunblock."

"I don't need any," Grant says.

"Yes, you do." I take off Baby's shirt.

"Sydney, put some sunblock on your brother's back, and make sure you rub it in good."

Ashlyn starts crying. I glance over at her. She's trying to get her shirt over her head but can't do it. "I'm never undressing again!" she cries.

"Come here, and I'll help you." It takes me a minute, but I manage to yank it off her abnormally large head—a cursed trait from my side of the family.

"Mom! Baby's going into the water!" Sydney shouts.

I jump up and snatch him before he dives in with his pants and shoes still on. "Not yet," I say. He fights and screams, and I'm grateful there's no one around to stare. There was a time (before kids) when I got the good kind of stares, but now I only get the nasty ones.

"Can you get Sydney's back?" I ask Grant. "And make sure you both get your arms and legs. Ashlyn, I'll get you. Come here."

I distract Baby with a book, giving me exactly forty seconds to work with. I know this because I've timed him. Working quickly, I dump a white glob of sun block into my hand and then rub it onto Ashlyn's skin. I finish, just as Baby tosses the book.

"Can we go to the lake now?" Grant asks.

"Sure. Don't forget your cups for the minnows."

The kids run toward the water. I start to walk with Baby to go in with them, when I hear a car pull up. It's my friend, Lynn. All four of her kids jump from the car and run to the water.

"Wait!" Lynn calls. "You need to take your clothes off and get sunblock on!" Three of them listen and stop, but her oldest boy keeps running until he jumps into the water, clothes and all.

Lynn growls.

"How's your morning going?" I ask.

"I'm here, so that's good, right?"

"Very." I dodge a blow from Baby's little fist.

"You?"

"Surviving."

"Uh-huh." She removes a bike and a couple of scooters from the back of her car. "I thought the kids might want to go to the skate park after they get bored of swimming."

"Good idea," I say, and help her carry her chairs and cooler.

"Should we let the babies go?" I ask Lynn after we've set up camp.

She looks at her eighteen-month-old in her arms. "I guess."

Together we set down our babies, whose legs are running before they hit the ground. They toddle to the water while we stay a safe distance behind.

My baby hits the water full speed. He naturally falls on all fours into the lake's shallow edge. His whole body shivers, and he looks like he's deciding whether or not to cry. When his baby friend, who was only a step away, falls into the water too and begins to wail, my baby decides that's the best solution.

Both of them cry hard, filling the lake with their tears. We pick them up and try to soothe them.

"I'm so glad that happened," Lynn says.

"Me too." Both of us know our babies will be more timid with the water now and not rush in.

Once they're calm, we set them back down. Like we suspected, they stick to the beach, preferring more to fill their diapers with sand than cold water.

Lynn and I sit in our chairs ten feet away and begin a conversation of our husbands' inability to place their dirty clothes into the laundry basket we've strategically placed at the foot of their bed. Our conversation is interrupted when Sydney and her friend run at us holding their plastic cups out.

"Look what we got," Sydney says.

"Did you catch some fish?" I ask.

She shakes her head and shows me her cup. I peer inside at the same time as Lynn. We both look at each other.

"You have got to be kidding," Lynn says and stands up, searching the ground.

I take the cup from Sydney and look at it again. The cup is full of broken glass. "Where did you get this?" I ask Sydney, hoping she'll say from somewhere far away.

"It's all over the beach. Isn't it pretty?"

Lynn and I walk over to the babies and pick them up.

"She's right. Look," Lynn says.

I don't have to look very hard. Every foot or so there's broken glass. "I thought they cleaned this place up."

"That's what I heard too," Lynn says, frowning.

I shake my head, and say, "I want to be reimbursed. Someone should pay me for my time and anguish to get the kids here."

"Call the mayor," Lynn suggests.

"I think I will. And instead of giving me money, I'll make him babysit my four kids all day in a small house, and then he'll know how important it is to have a nice park for kids to play at."

"That'll teach him," Lynn says. "Call him right when you get home. And let my kids come over too."

"Deal." We smile at each other. "So now what?" I say.

"Should we go over to the skate park?"

"Sure. Let's eat lunch first."

We slip our sandals on, and insist the kids do the same. We spread out blankets and begin to hand out lunch. When I open my grocery sack to retrieve the sandwiches I'd made earlier, I discover they've been stepped on.

"What's wrong?" Lynn asks when she notices my dismal expression.

"Another mindless sandwich killing."

"I have extras. Do you want some of ours?"

"No thanks," I say and remove the flat sandwiches from their baggies. "The kids can eat these. I'll tell them it's pita bread or something."

The children eat fast, all anxious to play at the skate park. I'm surprised when they don't complain about the sandwiches and even more surprised when they eat them all gone. I make a mental note to flatten the bread more often.

I'm gathering our garbage when I hear Lynn say to her youngest child, "Hey, sweetie. Whatchya got there? A pink toy?"

I turn around to see what her baby's holding. It's a small tube, plastic and pink. I take hold of Lynn's arm and freeze. "I don't think that's a toy."

She looks at her child, cocking her head. "Then what is it?"

While she's trying to figure out what I've already discovered, her child moves it toward his mouth. I rush to stop him, but just then Lynn figures it out. She screams and about knocks him over when she swats it from his hand. "Yuck! Yuck! Yuck! No! No! Gross! Disgusting!" She takes hold of his hands to keep him from touching anything.

"Wipe?" I ask.

"More like gasoline. I'm so grossed out!"

I hand her my package of wipes.

"Thanks." She proceeds to scrub her son's hands, pours water on them, and scrubs again, all the while editing her curse words for the children's sake.

When she's finished, I say, "Ready to go to the skate park?"

"Heck yes."

I drop off our picnic stuff in my SUV and then carry Baby toward the park, the children leading the way. They're well ahead of us, and by the time we catch up to them, they have already designated who gets to ride what toy.

Grant and his friend play on the scooter, Sydney and pal ride the bike, and Ashlyn and her little friend simply run up and down the skate ramp. The second we place the babies on the concrete, they rush to the edge of the park where somehow they've sensed an ant hill. I pretend I don't notice when Baby picks one up and licks it off his finger.

The bright sun hangs high in the sky; its light glares against the white pavement, and I have to squint just to see anything. But at least it's warm.

"I can't believe I've never come here before," I say. "The kids seem to be having a really good time."

Lynn nods. "My kids really like it. It's pretty much abandoned until the afternoon."

Grant zips expertly down a tall ramp; Sydney follows behind on a bike.

"You're baby likes the ants," Lynn says.

I glance the other way, toward the sound of a passing car blaring rap music. "Uh-huh."

"I mean he *really* likes them. He's popping them like jelly beans."

I meet her gaze. "I know. I'm just pretending I don't see it. Makes it easier, you know?"

She frowns.

"You think I should stop him?" I ask.

She thinks. "Ten minutes ago, I would've said yes, but ever since my son almost ate someone's tampon, ants don't seem so bad."

"I'll stop him in a minute," I say.

Ashlyn runs by me up a ramp. "This is fun, Mom!" she says.

I smile, glad the kids are having fun. There's nothing better than seeing your children happy.

"Do you want a turn, Mom?" Grant asks as he swerves from nearly hitting Ashlyn.

"No, thanks. I have to get your brother." I walk over and brush the ants off Baby's slobbery hand. "No more bugs for you. Why don't you play over here?" I guide him away from the ant hill. His little friend toddles after.

At that moment, something sinister must have passed over us—invisible flying demons or maybe the earth rotated into the Bermuda Triangle, because all of a sudden all hell breaks loose.

Grant's cry pierces the warm air. I run up a concrete hill and look over the skate park. Grant's on his knees at the bottom of a slope, rocking back and forth and clinging to his head. I rush over.

"What happened?" I ask.

His friend speaks fast. "We were racing down the ramp, and he ate it really bad. I heard his head hit the ground a mile away!"

I try to move Grant's hand to get a better look at his head, but he won't let me. "Let me see it, Grant."

He's crying so hard that he can't even speak.

I rub his back and am about to ask him again to see his head, when I hear two more screams. I stand up and search for the distress. Not far away I see that both Sydney and Ashlyn are on the ground crying. I pat Grant's back. "One sec, buddy."

I run over to the girls. Lynn is there trying to comfort them. "What happened?" I ask.

"They ran into each other," Lynn says. She's holding Ashlyn in one arm, and in the other her own child who's upset by all the crying. I take Ashlyn from her. "Are you okay?"

"Sydney tried to run me over with her bike!" she cries.

"I told you to move!" Sydney shouts through her tears.

"Mom!" Grant calls. He's still rocking back and forth.

While still holding Ashlyn, I scoop up Sydney with my free hand, holding her like a football, and shuffle toward Grant. *It could be worse*, I think. Baby could be crying too.

I freeze.

Where is Baby?

"Put me down," Sydney says.

"My arm hurts," Ashlyn says.

"Mom!" Grant cries again.

I whirl around in all directions searching for Baby. "Lynn!" I call. "Can you see my baby?"

She looks around too and points. "He's over there, almost to the parking lot!"

I'm about to drop the girls to race after Baby, when Lynn says, "I'll get him!" She dashes away, carrying her own baby, whose head looks like it's going to bounce off.

As soon as I reach Grant, I set the girls down. "All right. I need to see who's hurt worse. Ashlyn, let me see your arm."

She pushes up her sleeve and shows me a small patch of road burn. "You'll be fine. I don't see any blood and you seem to be using it okay. Sydney, what's wrong with you?"

"I hurt my knee."

"Can you still walk?"

She takes a step. "Barely."

"Then you're fine too."

"Grant, I need to see your head. Please let me look at it."

He slowly puts his hands down. I feel the back of his head and discover a huge goose egg. "You bumped it pretty good. How do you feel?"

"My head is killing me."

"Think you can walk to the car?"

"I think so."

I help him up, and let him lean into me.

Lynn arrives carrying her child and mine. "Caught him just in time. For having twelve-inch legs, he's fast!"

I take him from her. "Thanks," I say.

"Should we call it a day?" she says.

"I'm afraid so. It was fun while it lasted."

She nods in agreement.

Walking back to the car, I hold Baby in one arm, in the other hand I help Grant walk, and behind me, Ashlyn hangs onto the belt loop of my pants. Sydney tags along, sniffling because I can't help her too.

"Where's your husband?" Lynn asks.

"What's a 'husband'? Sounds like some new revolutionary tool that would solve all my problems."

She laughs. "At school?"

I unlock the car door. "I think he lives there."

"I've been in your shoes. It gets better."

"I hope so."

My kids are loaded up first. They aren't crying anymore, but they all look miserable. The warm car isn't helping. I jump into the driver's seat and look over at Lynn sitting in her car. I salute her and insert the keys into the ignition, but when I turn the ignition nothing happens. I try again. Still nothing.

This can't be happening.

I try again and again and again, hoping to hear any sounds of life. I even pound on the dashboard a few times, trying to jump-start its heart, but all I end up with is sweaty arm pits and a bruised fist.

There's a knock at my window. I roll the window down without looking over.

"Need some help?" Lynn asks.

"Possibly. I'm trying to figure out how to cut a hole out the bottom of this beast so I can just run it home. I really think the Flintstones were on to something."

"Technology is lame," she agrees. "Do you want to pop the hood?"

"Sure." I open the front hood and jump out of the car. Together we peer at the dirty engine.

"What do you think the problem is?" I ask her.

"Not a clue. Are we even looking at the right end?"

I touch a long hose. "I really should've taken auto mechanics in high school instead of drama."

"Let's try jumping it," Lynn suggests.

Fortunately she has jumper cables. Mine were taken out months ago to make room for a stroller. I make a mental note to examine my priorities later.

Within a few minutes, Lynn has Frankensteined my car. It sputters and comes to life. She removes the jumper cables and closes the hood. "What an adventure, eh?" she says.

I look at my dazed kids in the car. "It always is."

13

Grocery Wars

Every mother knows to pick their battles. I am no exception. Some battles I don't mind fighting, like insisting my kids eat all their dinner, or limiting TV time. But there are others I avoid altogether. They are the ones that are the most bloody and violent. They leave their victims scarred for life, including innocent bystanders.

I've just changed Baby when a battle of epic proportions stares me in the face: *I've used the last diaper.*

I don't know how I missed it. I'm always so careful. My brain begins turning wheels that have never been turned before as I desperately try to think of a way to avoid the grocery store battle. I never go to the store with all the kids. It's a suicide mission. Every mother knows that.

With Baby in arms, I round up the other kids from the four corners of my home for a family meeting. When they are sitting semi-still, I say, "I will pay five dollars to whoever can find me a diaper. Ten if you can find two. I need one to get Baby through the night, and one for the morning."

"Serious?" Grant asks, wide-eyed.

"Uh-huh. I want you to look everywhere. In the car, closets, toy box, dog house. Anywhere you think a diaper might be. And hurry."

They scatter.

Ten minutes later, Baby and I sort through a big pile of crap the kids have dumped on the kitchen table. From the looks of it, there are no diapers, but plenty of items they think can replace one: a towel, a baby blanket, newspaper, cardboard box, a dress, three sponges, and a cork. It's hopeless. The grocery store is my only option.

"I want all children in the living room," I call.

I wait a few minutes, but no one comes.

I try again. "I want everyone in the living room right now, or I'll tell your father!"

This time they come running. I place Baby next to them. "I need you all to sit down in front of me and fold your arms."

They quiet down, probably thinking I'm about to say something profound. I pace in front of them, arms crossed. "As you well know, I am out of diapers. And this presents a serious problem, because there's only one thing I can do. Can anyone tell me what that is?"

All hands shoot into the air.

"Yes, Grant?"

"Tape Baby to the toilet."

"Wrong. Sydney?"

"Let Baby sleep in the tub."

This idea gives me pause. "Not bad, but too many logistic problems. Ashlyn?"

"Can I go to the bathroom?"

"In a minute." I pull up a kitchen chair and sit in front of them. "Here's the deal. I have to get diapers, and the only place to get them is the grocery store, and since Dad's not here, I have to take you guys."

The room explodes with cheers. The kids are jumping up and down, hugging each other, and I think Grant is crying for joy. I wave my arms, trying to silence them. "Calm down! It's not like we're going to Disneyland. It's just the grocery store."

Sydney's hugging me. "But you never let us go!"

"I can't wait to see what I get!" Grant says.

Ashlyn's eyes are big. "I'm going to get a Barbie, a dress, a new bike—"

"Stop! Everyone sit down and be quiet!"

The kids return to their spots, but their legs still twitch and their bodies rock side to side.

"Seriously, guys. Calm down. No one is getting anything. I only need diapers." I pause, thinking. "And milk and bread. In and out. Got it?"

They nod and smile, but I notice an odd gleam in their eyes.

"I'm *serious*," I repeat. "Now let's go over the rules. Number one: no yelling. We speak with a quiet and respectful voice, so that means no fighting. Rule number two: no staring. We are not to stare or point or comment at anything or anyone who looks different. Rule number three: no asking for things. Come to think of it, maybe we should just make a rule of no talking."

"How 'bout we just put bags over our heads," Grant mumbles.

"Great idea, Grant, but I don't have any brown bags, and plastic bags would be inhumane. Rule number four: no touching *anything*. Keep your hands to yourself. Rule number five: absolutely no running. Stay next to me at all times. And finally, rule number six: obey me!" I look at each of them. "Do you all understand the rules?"

They nod, but still there's that gleam.

"Stand to attention, please," I say. "Good. Now repeat after me. I solemnly swear—" they look at each other and giggle, but repeat my words— "to pretend to be good children for one whole hour. I will not yell, fight, or stare. I will not ask for things, and I will not touch any object, even if I think it asks me. And most of all, I will obey my mother, my Queen, or suffer a most horrible fate."

Ashlyn frowns. "What's a *horrible fate*?"

I pause. "Think worms and bugs and four-headed monsters."

"I don't want a horrible fate," she says.

"And nor should you, so be good." I pick up Baby and remove a ball of carpet fuzz from his mouth. "Grant, get the diaper bag ready. The rest of you get your shoes on and meet me in the car in five. Go!"

Fifteen minutes later we're sitting in the car as it idles in the driveway.

"Aren't we going to go?" Sydney asks.

"Just a second. I'm saying a prayer."

"For what?"

"Strength." I pause. "Amen. Okay, let's go."

It's not long before we're at the grocery store, scouring the parking lot for a spot close to the entrance. Somewhere between my house and the store it has decided to rain, and none of my kids have jackets. "See any spots?" I ask.

"There's one!" Grant says, pointing to the back of the lot.

"Over there by McDonald's," Sydney adds with hope.

"Any by the grocery store?"

"I don't see any."

I give up and decide to park in the back next to the cart corral. Hopefully this will help me avoid the inevitable argument about who gets to return the grocery cart. I turn around in my seat. "When I say go, let's bolt. Ready? Set. Go!" I open the door, close it, open Baby's door, get him out of the car seat, and then close the door behind us—all in about ten seconds. I walk quickly around the car, expecting to see three kids waiting for me. There are none.

Their door is open, but all three of them are staring up into dark sky while rain pours on top of Baby and me. "Come on! Let's go!"

"But it's raining," Ashlyn says.

"There are worse things than rain. Remember 'most horrible fate'?"

She jumps from the car, followed by the others. Carrying Baby in one arm and holding Ashlyn's hands with the other, I lead the way inside.

"Can we take this cart?" Sydney asks while I try to dry Baby off.

I turn around. She's standing in front of a blue grocery cart styled as a truck. "I guess, but there's only room for Baby and one other inside."

At the same time, all three kids yell, "I get it!"

"Shhhh! Settle down. You'll have to take turns. Ashlyn's the youngest so she gets to first."

"What! That's no fair. I'm the oldest," Grant complains.

"But not the cutest," I say, smiling. I set Baby in the front seat behind the rubber steering wheel and buckle him in. Immediately, his mouth goes for the wheel. I place my hand over it just in time. Instead, he bites my hand. "Ouch!" I exclaim. Even though his Baby teeth are scraping against my flesh, I don't remove my hand for fear he'll contract some horrible disease from the pretend steering wheel. "Grant, get me one of those grocery cart wipes. Quick!" I expect to see blood any second.

"They're out, Mom."

I frown. Not a whole lot I can do now. I withdraw my hand. "Have at it, kid, but if you get RSV, you're on your own. Hop in Ashlyn." Ashlyn slides in next to Baby. "Let's make this quick, guys, and remember the rules."

I'm not even ten steps down the first aisle when rule number four is broken. Grant shoves Sydney into a display of Twinkies almost knocking them over.

"Are you serious, Grant?" I ask.

"She called me dumb!"

"I don't care if she called you a brainless, hairless monkey who eats his own poo, you don't shove your sister," I hiss, looking at each of them. "Both of you get a strike for breaking rule number four and one. Now be good!"

They grudgingly start walking again, ugly scowls deforming their faces. I should've made a rule number seven: pretend to be happy.

I turn down the next aisle. Baking goods. I could really use a chocolate cake. Walking in front of the cart, Sydney and Grant are whispering—never a good thing. "What are you guys talking about?" I ask.

They turn around. "Nothing. Just making up," Grant says, but the moment he turns back, he's whispering to Sydney again. Suddenly, he shouts, "Three!" And both of them begin sprinting down the aisle.

"Noooooo!" I call, but it's too late. They reach the end just as an elderly lady turns the corner. Grant tries to stop, but ends up tripping, which turns out to be a good thing because his bare knees sliding against the linoleum floor stop him just before he plows into the woman.

I rush forward. "I am so sorry," I tell her, and then four more words burst from my mouth. They're the words I always say to explain away any troubles in my life: "I have four kids."

"Why were you late?"

"I have four kids."

"You forgot the cupcakes."

"I have four kids."

"Did you know you were speeding?"

"I have four kids."

My excellent excuse has gotten me out of some nasty situations. The older woman with graying hair and dark eyes smiles sympathetically. "I understand. I have four too," she says.

I return her smile as she walks by, but the second she passes my lips jerk as tight as my eyebrows. I grab Grant and Sydney's arms and bend down, my nose inches from theirs. "What were you two *thinking*?"

"We were racing to see who could get you the milk first," Grant says.

Sydney's eyes are brimming. "We were only trying to help."

I stand up and inhale deeply.

"Sorry, Mom," Grant says.

"Yeah, sorry," Sydney adds.

"Whatever. Just don't break the rules again. Okay?"

They nod.

I return to the cart just in time to catch Baby as he's falling from the cab of the plastic truck. "What happened, Ashlyn?"

"He got out of his seat belt."

"And how did he do that?"

"I undid it."

"Why?"

"I want to drive."

"Well you don't get to. Undo him again and you'll have to go to bed early. Okay?"

She's playing with a cake mix box from off the shelf.

"Are you hearing me?" I ask.

"Can we get this?"

I snatch it from her. "Listen to me, please. Don't unbuckle your brother, quit touching things, and stop asking for things. Got it?"

"Fine." Her bottom lip sticks out.

"Good." I push the cart again, quicker this time. I make it to the milk aisle without another incident, but once there, Sydney insists on trading spots with Ashlyn. I'm busy removing a gallon of milk, when I hear Ashlyn yell, "Don't touch me! Mom!"

I turn around, along with everyone else on the aisle. "Stop it! Both of you. Sydney, don't touch her, and Ashlyn don't yell. Remember the rules?"

"But she pulled my shirt!" Ashlyn yells again.

I bend down to her, really close, so she can see the fire in my eyes. "Stop yelling. Use your quiet voice, do you understand?" She nods, but she's staring at Sydney so hard I wouldn't be surprised to see Sydney's hair fall out.

"Look at me, Ashlyn."

She looks, sort of. One eyes is on me and the other remains on Sydney. I admit, I'm a little freaked out. I snap my fingers in front of her face. "Hey, Crazy-eye. Look at me." Finally both eyes focus on me. "It's Sydney's turn. You need to get out." She opens her mouth to speak. "No arguing," I interrupt. "Remember rule number six: obey your mother?"

Her face scrunches together like a rolled up newspaper ready to swat the first thing that speaks. I don't say a word, but I do take her firmly by the arm and pull her from the car. Sydney slides in before Ashlyn's seat has a chance to get cold.

Once again, I start forward toward the bread section, but when I realize Ashlyn's not with us, I turn back around. She's standing twenty feet away, arms folded to her chest. "Get over here, Ashlyn."

"I'm not moving," she says.

"Fine. Have fun sleeping here tonight with the eight-legged produce monster," I say and walk off.

It takes less than a second for her to come crying after me. Her wails are worse than a siren.

"I'm sorry," I say to everyone around me. "I have four kids."

They smile and move on. I take hold of Ashlyn. "Stop crying right now or I'm going to take you to the car."

"Then take me."

Inwardly, I curse. She called my bluff. "I will when we're finished and you're not going to like it."

I move away from her, glancing back every now and then to make sure she's following.

"Grant, pick out some bread, please," I say.

"Don't get any with oat stuff on top," Sydney says. "Or the

brown kind." She's holding Baby back from trying to hit her. "Mom, can you tell Baby to stop?"

"Be good, Baby," I say. A little ways down from the bread, I notice potato chips. I walk down and grab a bag of sour cream and cheddar. This will be my reward, I decide.

Back at the cart, Grant has picked out bread so white it's practically glowing. But I don't say anything. He accomplished the task without any fighting or complaining. That's all I can hope for.

I push the cart to the end of the aisle, then stop. Something's not right. I look around. Definitely, not right. I stick my head into the plastic truck and count only Baby and Sydney. I stand up. Grant's just ahead, poking his finger into a bag of hamburger buns. "Where's Ashlyn?" I ask.

Nobody answers.

"Grant!"

He looks at me.

"Where's Ashlyn?"

He glances around. "She was just right here."

I maneuver the cart out of the aisle and start walking, scanning each passing row, but I don't see her. "Ashlyn!" I call. "Grant, run ahead and see if you can find her."

"But I'm not supposed to run."

"This time you can."

He dashes off.

I circle four different rows before Grant meets up with me again.

"I didn't find her, Mom."

My heart drops and suddenly it's hard to breathe. "She's got to be here." I keep moving up and down the rows. I don't let my thoughts wander to all the horrible possibilities. *I'll find her*, I keep telling myself. She's here. She has to be. But several minutes later, panic sets in.

I find a store clerk at an empty check out station. "I can't find my daughter," I say, trying to keep my voice steady.

"Are we *finally* done?" I hear a familiar voice say.

I look around. "Ashlyn?"

Nothing.

"Did you hear that Grant?"

Grant too is turning in circles, looking everywhere. "It was definitely Ashlyn."

"So you're missing a child?" the male clerk with a thin mustache asks.

"Yeah, but I just heard her, but can't see her."

"Ma'am?" the guy says, smirking.

"Yes?"

"Have you looked under the truck?"

"Under?"

He nods.

I bend over. Just beneath the blue truck is about an eight-inch space that some yahoo inventor thought would be a good idea. *What an idiot.* No mom would ever use the space, let alone see it, but a small child with a bone to pick would find it the perfect hiding place.

I yank Ashlyn out so fast, the store clerk says, "Whoa, I don't think she meant any—"

I shut him up with by best Medusa look then turn to Ashlyn. "I have been looking everywhere for you. Do you know how much you worried me?"

"Why?"

"Because I thought you'd been kidnapped. Don't ever hide from me again, do you understand?"

"Yes."

I turn to the rest of my kids. "Rule number seven: no hiding!" I pick up Ashlyn. "And you my dear, get to sit in the cart. Just don't step on any food." I give her a big hug before I set her down and then push aside the few items I have to make room for her.

I take a deep breath. "Should we try this again?"

Grant raises his hand and then slashes it down like a sword. "For Narnia!" he calls and starts marching forward.

Sydney and Ashlyn giggle, and even I can't help but smile.

For the next several minutes, the kids are pretty good. Just minor bickering, nothing I can't handle, but Baby's growing increasingly upset. He's pounding on the steering wheel and shouting what sounds like curse words in an alien language. When his behavior elicits more stares than I can handle, I pull him from the cart and hold him, while also trying to steer. This proves too difficult. "Grant, will you push?"

He eagerly agrees.

"It's not a real car," I say. "You know that right?"

"I'm not five, Mom."

"But you're a boy, so that's pretty much the same thing. Just watch where you're going, okay?"

"This is easy, Mom. Chill out."

His words strike me in the back. I turn around. "Don't say that to me. Only your father can tell me to *chill out* and even then only in emergencies."

"Why?"

"Because until he, or you, has four children ripped from

your gut, stayed up all night for days on end, becomes trapped in an abusive cycle of laundry and dishes, been puked on, peed on, pooped on, and has to eat their meals in under one minute or risk starvation, you can't ever tell me to 'chill out.' Got it?"

His lip quivers, but he quickly nods.

I smile and give him a hug with my free arm. "Good. You'll make a great husband one day."

"I don't want to get married," he mumbles as he pushes the cart.

"You'll get tricked into it," I say.

"Mom, can I have Captain Crunch?" Sydney asks from within the truck.

I'd almost forgotten she was there. "No, we have cold cereal at home. What are you doing in there anyway? You're awfully quiet."

"Coloring."

I head toward the Baby section, glad Sydney has something to do. *At least I have one good child*, I think.

When I turn the corner, I freeze. At the end of the walkway the toy aisles begin. It's a beautiful sight, even I can't deny that. Big, fluffy and bright stuffed animals sit on top of the shelves. They have huge grins and seem to be waving directly at me. Below them, Barbies dance, army men battle gaily, mechanical dogs yip and yap, and Luke Skywalker saves the universe.

The toys have momentarily hypnotized me, but I snap out of it when Grant runs the cart into the back of my heel. "Ouch," I say and limp forward. "Watch where you're going!"

But he doesn't respond. He, along with all the other kids,

including Baby, have fallen under the toys' spell. They stand with mouths open, completely still, and I know there's nothing I can do to break their trance.

"Toys," Ashlyn whispers.

"Barbies," Sydney says louder.

"Army dudes," Grant practically yells.

Baby shouts and slaps the top of my head over and over.

Losing all fear of their mother's rules, the kids race toward the toys, arms flailing in the air, crying for joy. The baby wiggles fiercely until he reaches the floor. He toddles after them, pure bliss blanketing his face.

"Stop!" I call, but my words disappear into the wake of their glee. I grab the cart and hurry after them, but by the time I get there, all four kids carry toys in each arm and are speaking at once.

"Can I get these?" Ashlyn asks.

Grant pulls on me from behind. "Mom, you totally have to get this for me. Cooper has one and we—"

Sydney's in front of me saying, "Please, Mom, can I have this? I finished my book and you promised—"

Not far off, Baby's ripping objects off shelves and throwing them everywhere, all the while laughing.

The sounds of all my children ruthlessly pound into me. Their faces are distorted, and I can't recognize any of them. It's as if they've suddenly become possessed by the souls of toy-demons.

"Silence!" I roar.

Every kid in the aisle stops and stares at the shouting monster with a red face and frizzy hair. "You don't *need* all this," I cry. "You can be happy without all the bright colors, the bleeps and bloops, and shiny metal. You have to stay strong. Don't let their outer appearance fool you!"

The kids look right through me to a toy just beyond, and I know I've lost. I was defeated the moment I stepped into the store. I'm out-numbered and out-gunned. My usual disciplinary tactics can't work here. At home if they acted like this, I could put them in a time out or send them to bed. Even in public, I've dropped everything to "teach" a lesson, once leaving a cart full of groceries when a child was naughty. But I can't do that now. I need diapers.

My head drops and I raise the white flag. "If you guys promise to be good the rest of the time, I'll let you pick out a toy under three dollars, okay?"

They all give me big hugs. "Thanks, Mom!"

Not long after I'm placing the largest box of diapers I can find into the cart. Each kid is playing quietly with their toys. Baby's especially happy with his toy SpongeBob cell phone. Every second he pushes a button and an obnoxious voice says, "More soup for your arm pit?"

We're at the checkout, when Ashlyn points to a man and says loudly, "Mom, look a cowboy!" And then she gets really excited when she sees a dark-skinned man behind him. "And he looks like an Indian! Are they going to kill each other?"

I don't remind her that she's just broken rule number two. None of the rules matter after a battle's been lost. After paying for the items, I push the cart slowly to the car, despite the rain. The kids don't notice anything but their toys. Once they're in the car, I return the cart. Before I leave, I stick my head into the plastic truck to make sure we got everything. What I see almost makes me burst into tears. The inside of it has been decorated with fairies, flowers, and ballerinas. And on the top is scribbled a monster with frizzy hair and a red face.

I hadn't just lost a battle, I'd been slaughtered.

14

The Monster Within

Friedrich Nietzche once said, "Battle not with monsters lest you become one."

There is a monster I battle daily. And most of the time I lose. For that battle turns me into a fire-eyed, crazy screaming monster.

In many cultures this monster is revered and families huddle around it as it lies on the table, adorned with colorful dishes and tantalizing smells. Others I know welcome this monster into their homes, even going as far as to share it with others. But in my home, the monster is feared. I hate what he does to me, and only I am able to see him for what he really is. What is this monster's name?

Dinner.

It's almost five o'clock in the afternoon. Ashlyn finds her way into my office and stares. I ignore her and try to finish up a proposal for a customer.

She still stares.

And then sighs.

And then knocks her knee repeatedly into my desk.

I stop typing and look at her. "What's up?"

"I'm hungry."

The monster rears its head.

"Already? Didn't you just have lunch?"

She smacks her lips as if trying to taste any leftovers. "I don't remember."

I start typing again. "Go downstairs and get a cracker out of the pantry."

"I already had one. I'm hungry for big food."

The monster growls.

I glance at the clock. "Fine. I'll be down in just a second."

"Can you come now?"

I glance at the unfinished paperwork scattered on my desk. Fail at my business or fail with the kids? I stand up and take her hand. "What do you want for dinner?"

She shrugs and asks, "What dinosaur do I look like?"

I walk down the stairs with her. "A cute-a-saurus," I say and return her smile. I find the other children in the living room. Baby is still napping. "What do you guys want for dinner?"

Grant keeps his eyes on the TV. "Steak."

"Crepes," Sydney says.

Ashlyn tugs on my hand. "I'll have brownies."

The monster snaps its jaws. I turn around and head into my room to find my husband. He's in the shower getting ready for work. I stick my head into the steam. I can't see him, but I know he's in there somewhere. "What do you want for dinner?" I ask.

"Anything. But it will have to be quick. I have to go in early."

"Spaghetti?"

"No. I already have indigestion."

"Eggs and toast?"

"Sick of it."

"Ham sandwich?"

"Had that for lunch."

"I thought you said you'd eat anything."

His head appears from within the fog. "I will. Just make it, and I'll eat it."

I frown and close the shower door.

"Mom! Baby's awake!" Grant's voice calls.

I resist the urge to slump to the floor, despite the fact that I feel myself transforming into the very monster I hate.

Letting Baby cry, I walk into the kitchen and open my fridge. Three eggs, four sweating pieces of bologna, broccoli that looks more like a haunted forest, and a package of hot dogs. Not a lot to work with.

I go to the pantry, hoping to miraculously find something new—a loaf of bread and some fish would be nice. It's happened before, why not to me? But all I find is crumbled up crackers on the floor. That's new.

"When are we eating?" Sydney asks.

I turn around. "Soon. Hey, will you watch Baby while I make dinner?'

Sydney scowls. "He doesn't like me."

"Impossible.

"He always hits me."

"He's playing."

"With my face?"

"Can you just get him?"

She huffs.

"By the way," I ask. "What do you want for dinner?"

"Mac and cheese."

"We had that for dinner last night."

"Add tuna this time."

"We'll see. Just get the baby." Secretly, I already know we aren't having tuna because I hate opening the can. My fingers smell fishy for weeks.

I walk into the living room. "Grant, what do you want for dinner? We don't have steak."

The TV holds his attention better than I ever have. "Ramen noodles."

"We had that for lunch."

He shrugs.

"Ashlyn, what do you want?"

"Crepes."

"We don't have enough eggs."

"But that's what I want!" she whines.

I ignore her and return to the kitchen. Surely I can find something. Sydney appears with the baby in her arms. He's hitting her face.

"No, no!" I say. "Just put him down, Sydney."

She sets him down and storms away. Baby cries. *I can do this*, I think. And hope. "Grant, turn off the TV and help me with Baby," I ask.

I return to the pantry and scan the shelves. There must be something I can use. Cans of green beans, corn, and applesauce tell me I'm hard pressed.

Baby finds me. He wraps his arms around my legs and wails. "Mama! Mama!" It's the only word he knows. That wouldn't be such a problem if he knew how to say it quietly, but he doesn't.

"Mom!" Ashlyn yells.

I walk back to the fridge, sliding Baby with me. "What?" I emphasize the "T." The monster begins to show its ugly face.

Ashlyn's arms are crossed. "Grant's not letting me sit on the couch."

I look at Grant. "Grant, I asked you to turn off the TV and help me with Baby."

"What?" He can't hear me over the crying baby and the television.

"Turn off the TV!" I shout.

He clicks the power button on the remote. "How come you're so mad?" he asks.

I calm down. "Just help me, please?"

He picks up Baby. "Wanna play Legos?"

"No Legos," I say. "He'll choke."

"So what are we supposed to do?"

"Go read him a story."

Grant walks off; the baby's hitting the top of his head and screaming "Mama!"

I open the fridge door and grab the first thing I see: sour cream. I remove the lid. A white lump swims in a sea of oily juice. I check the expiration date: two weeks ago. Close enough.

Ashlyn appears from nowhere. "I'm hungry."

"That's what I keep hearing. Why don't you help me? You can stir."

She smiles. "Really?"

"Sure." I pull two pots out of a cupboard. From the pantry I remove a can of chicken soup and a box of rice.

"What are we having?" she asks.

"Something magical." I fill the pan with water and set it

on the stove to boil. In the other pan I dump the soup and the rest of the sour cream; it slides out like a snail from its shell.

"I'm not eating that," Ashlyn says.

"Me either," Sydney says. She's sitting on a chair next to Ashlyn. Where did she come from?

"You'll love it, I promise," I say, nervously looking around for another child. When I feel sure there are no more, I look back at Sydney and Ashlyn. "This is the same meal Cinderella had on her wedding night."

"Then I don't want it," Grant says appearing behind me. He hands me Baby who is still crying. "He tore up a book."

"Great." I pat Baby's back, and finally he's quiet.

"Can you kids set the table, please?" None of them move. "Hello? Did you guys hear me?"

Blank stares, but at least they're looking at me. I speak slowly. "Will you please set the table?"

They moan and groan but move.

With Baby on my hip, I begin to stir the funky-looking concoction in the pan. In my other pot, steam rises up, and Baby's fighting to reach it. "No! Don't touch. Hot! Ouch!" I attempt to show him how hot the lid is when I accidentally touch it. "Ouch!" I move to the sink and run my finger under cold water. Baby laughs.

"Mom, Grant's not helping," Sydney says.

"Grant, please help."

"How much longer?" Ashlyn asks as she walks out from my bedroom.

I open my mouth to answer but notice something. Her face is shining like its wet.

"What's on your face?" I ask her.

"Nothing."

"Ashlyn, what did you put on your face?"

Sydney leans in to get a closer look. "She smells funny."

"Come here, Ashlyn," I say.

She hesitantly steps forward. I bend down to inspect the slime. It's a thin coat of gloss, and she smells like she's stuck her face in a pine tree. I use a tone: "Ashlyn, what did you do?"

"Nothing."

"Tell me right now or you're going to time out."

While she thinks about it, I straighten and stir the food. After a few seconds, I say, "Well?"

She looks down. "I put daddy's armpit stuff on my face."

"Deodorant?"

She shrugs.

If I wasn't still struggling to hold Baby and trying to cook dinner, I would've laughed, but my white brew has begun to boil, and I don't think it's supposed to do that. I make a mental note to laugh later. I look at her. "Where's the deodorant?"

"In my room."

"Can you please put it back in Daddy's bathroom and then wash your face?"

She nods and walks away.

Just then I smell something. And it's not my almost burnt food. "This can't be happening," I mumble. I lift Baby and smell his bum. "Jiminy good crap Christmas!"

"What's wrong, Mom?" Grant asks. He's playing with Legos on the kitchen table that is supposed to be set. He sees my expression and looks at the Legos and then back at me. He must value his safety more than his teetering Star Wars cruiser because he says, "How can I help?"

I inhale deeply and slowly let the air out. "Can you stir the food while I change Baby?"

"Sure." He walks over and takes the spoon from me.

I carry Baby to his room, careful to avoid pressing on his bum, and open his bedroom door. I glance around, taking in the sight before me. The room is a wreck. Books have been thrown everywhere, there's a fort on top of the crib, and I swear every stuffed animal we own has been dressed in a diaper. "Girls!" I yell, exposing monster teeth. "Get in here right now!"

They are familiar with this tone and come running, even Grant. "Uh-oh," Grant says when he sees the mess.

"Who did this?" I ask.

The girls point at each other.

I begin to count to ten, but only make it to three. In a scary base voice, I say, "Clean this up right now."

The monster has spoken, and the girls know better than to disobey it. They spring into action.

Meanwhile, I remove a diaper off a stuffed animal, grab the wipes, and go into the living room to change the baby. I set him on the floor and pull down his pants. I'm not prepared for what I encounter. Bubbling out the top and sides of his diaper like the brewing pot of Macbeth's witches is a greenish brown liquid. It looks and smells toxic. "Grant, get me a towel!" I'm holding Baby's legs in the air, and he's not liking the position. He begins to wail and twist his body back and forth. "Hurry, Grant!"

When Grant finally comes, I'm holding Baby upside down in the air. Baby's laughing.

"Can I be next?" Grant asks.

I grunt. "I'm not swinging him. I'm trying to keep him from getting poo on the carpet."

"Oh." Grant lays the towel on the floor.

I set Baby down and proceed to change him. It's a painfully slow process, but I'm almost done.

And then he starts going again.

I lift his legs back into the air and wait. It's during this moment that I reflect on my past life. Only eight years ago, in fact. Specifically the time my husband and I traveled to Italy where we walked the cobblestone streets of Lecce, slept in until whenever (who needed to keep track of time?), and enjoyed a quiet meal with a kind old lady who'd gotten the local town hunter to kill a rabbit for our feast. Life was simple then. Stress-free and quiet.

And never stunk. Both metaphorically and literally.

The steady stream of poop slowly subsides. When I begin to wipe him, Baby squirms again, trying hard to turn on his belly. "When did you get so strong?" I ask as I wrestle to get him to hold still. It takes me a few minutes, but I complete the task.

"Mom?" Grant asks from the kitchen. I hear the hesitancy in his voice.

I roll up the dirty towel. "What is it?"

"Should there be brown stuff floating in this sauce?"

"Noooooo!" I rush over although it feels as if I'm running in water. I look into the pot. "Son of a—"

"What's wrong?" Grant interrupts just in time.

My lip quivers. "The sauce burned." I turn the burner off and stare into the swirling mess. Behind me, Baby's gotten into a drawer of cake pans and is banging them together. If he were taller, I'd ask him to knock me over the head with one.

Over the banging, Ashlyn shouts, "My stomach hurts. When are we eating?"

"In just a minute." I grab a spoon and scoop out several burned pancake-like spots. What's left can be passed off as pepper. I look at the table. "Why isn't the table set?"

The children all look at one another and then back at me. "Set it now!"

I turn around to grab the salt, but trip on a wandering Baby. My elbow hits the counter, and my knee smacks into Baby's head. We both start crying.

"Mom! Grant stabbed me with a fork!" Sydney yells.

"It's a spoon, dork-face," Grant says.

"Mom, I'm hungry!" Ashlyn whines.

From the bottom of my toes, I feel the monster shake as it rises higher and higher. If one put their ear to the floor they'd hear it coming. It rumbles low like an oncoming freight train. Blood rushes to my face and out the monster comes. In a loud, scary demon voice, I yell, "All of you in time-out now!"

They freeze as if the cold air blasting from my lungs has turned them to ice. "Move!"

They scatter into the living room, each one of them choosing their own time-out spot. I stomp to the baby's room and place him as gently as possible (if I don't mentally take note on how I'm setting him down, I'm afraid I'll throw him like a baseball) into his crib. I slam his door to try and block his cries, then return to the kitchen where I place my hands on the counter, head down, and breathe. I hate losing control.

I take a minute to collect myself and to try to banish the monster festering inside me. *Bedtime is in two hours*, I tell myself. I snatch a handful of chocolate chips from my baking drawer and pop them into my mouth. *I can do this.* I finish set-ting the table. The whole time my kids are quiet, even though I see them attempting to spell words to each other with their hands.

Just as I'm about to call everyone to dinner, my husband opens the bedroom door and walks into the kitchen. After using his sock to wipe off shower water from his face, he looks around. The table is set, dinner is ready, and the kids are sitting quietly on the couch. "How come the kids are always good for you?" he asks.

The monster snorts.

15

Bargaining with God

You never think it will happen to you—a tragic, heart-wrenching event that you see only other people go through. But then a rock's suddenly thrown into the loud grinding wheels of your life and it comes to a screeching, groaning halt. You question all that you believe and end up feeling helpless and vulnerable.

This happens to me after I discover a strange dimpled, discoloration at the small of Ashlyn's back. She is nine months old.

"It's probably nothing," I say to the doctor as we both stare down at Ashlyn's bare back, "but since I'm already here for her immunizations, I might as well show you."

He runs his fingers over it. "I'm not sure what it is, but I'd like to refer you to a dermatologist."

"Okay," I answer, not thinking anything of it. I'm so unconcerned that I forget to mention the appointment to my husband.

Two weeks later, another doctor looks at Ashlyn's lower back. "When did you first notice it?" he asks.

"Around six months old, but I thought it was just a skin discoloration, but as she's gotten older, it's started to dimple a little." I watch closely as the doctor pushes on and around the area. Ashlyn clings to me with a worried look on her face, but when I smile, she smiles back.

The doctor sits up. "I'd like her to get an MRI."

This surprises me. "Really? How come?"

"It could be nothing . . . or it could be a tumor at the base of her spine. I've seen it before."

I swallow. "A tumor?"

"Yes, see here?" He lifts Ashlyn's shirt up again and points to the dimpled area. "A growing tumor could be causing that dimpled effect."

"And what about the discoloration?" I ask.

"It's related to the tumor," he says and goes into a lengthy lecture on how the tumor could be affecting that part of the body.

I try to focus on what he's saying, as I know Aaron will want to know everything, but all I can think of is asking one question: "How serious is this?"

"Honestly, I can't say until she's had an MRI. But if there is a tumor, then we'll want to do a biopsy to see if it's benign or malignant."

He says more, but I'm staring down at my perfectly healthy-looking child. *She's fine*, I tell myself. *Stuff like this happens to other people, not me.*

After scheduling our next appointment, I say good-bye to the doctor. The next thing I remember is walking through my front door, but I can't remember how I got there. I lay down Ashlyn for a nap and then sit across from her crib and just stare, not allowing my mind to think of all the possibilities.

I'm still sitting there when Aaron comes home an hour later. I give Ashlyn a quick kiss and then sneak to go tell Aaron the news. I keep a brave face, as does he, and then we don't mention it again. Neither of us can bear to think of the future.

Until after the MRI.

Ashlyn does have a tumor and it's grown all around the base of her spine, even tethering with her spinal cord. The news feels like a hot screwdriver to the heart, twisting and burning. Aaron asks the doctor a lot of questions, but I just sit there, stone faced, asking silent questions to a different kind of doctor, one that I hope will remove the pain from my heart. *Why her? A small innocent child who has so much to offer the world? It doesn't make sense. I'm the better candidate. What have I done that's so special or worthy-making? I should be the one to suffer, not her.*

I don't tell my husband how I'm feeling because I can see in his pain-etched face that he's feeling the same way. It's hard to comfort each other when you both feel extreme guilt and sorrow.

We spend as much time with Ashlyn and the other children as possible. Cleaning, laundry, meetings, and appointments suddenly aren't important anymore. We stay home mostly, spending every second together, waiting for a consultation with a neurosurgeon at Primary Children's Medical Center in Salt Lake City.

When the time comes, the neurosurgeon tells us he'd like to operate immediately. First to remove the tumor, and second to determine if the tumor is benign or malignant. He follows this up by saying there's also a chance the surgery could paralyze her. He assures us he will do the best he can, but his words do not comfort us.

The night before surgery, we take Ashlyn into the hospital's lab for blood work. A nurse leads us into a small room where she examines Ashlyn's veins. "We're going to need several vials so this will probably be hard on her."

"Just do what you have to do," Aaron says. Any emotions he may have been feeling have been left outside in the cold. Mine, however, followed me in.

I hold my daughter's hand tight, my stomach twisting.

"Can you lay down, sweetie?" the nurse asks Ashlyn.

Ashlyn's eyes dart back and forth between mine and Aaron's. We smile encouragingly.

"It's okay," I say and help lay her down.

The nurse ties a rubber strip on her arm, and then looks at me. "Can you hold her arms down? And you," she looks at Aaron, "her legs?"

We nod and get into position.

"Mama?" Her small voice sucks the air from the room and my lungs.

I smooth her hair. "It's okay. This will only hurt for a second."

The nurse slides the needle into her little arm. Ashlyn immediately cries out and begins to thrash. She's stronger than we all expected, and we tighten our grip.

The nurse grunts and I see her wiggling the needle into Ashlyn's flesh. "I can't find it." I can barely hear her over Ashlyn's cries.

"Mama! Mama!"

I whisper in her ear to try and calm her down, but all she understands is her parents are holding her down while a stranger causes her pain. Her terrified eyes burn into mine, and my already-wounded heart bleeds.

"Let's try the other arm," the nurse says, clearly frustrated. We start over.

Same results. Ashlyn screams and we hold her down. I sing in her ear, then try to tell her a story, but she can't hear me.

The nurse brings in a colleague. "We can't find it in her arms, so we're going to try her feet."

"Can't we let the doctor do this in the morning?" I say, my insides trembling.

The nurse shakes her head. "I'm sorry, but we need the blood work tonight."

She then tells us to take our positions again. I hold the top of Ashlyn, my face pressed against hers. She's clinging to my neck, screaming my name. I can't hold the tears in any longer and they spill down my cheeks. When the second nurse informs us that she too cannot find a vein and that they'd like to try the other foot, I clench my fists, ready to punch the freckles from her face. Aaron turns to me, his face unrecognizable. "You need to leave. We'll take care of this."

I look down at Ashlyn whose arms are reaching for me.

"Go now," his cold voice says. "She will be fine, but you need to go."

I look into the eyes of a stranger, wondering how he managed to disassociate himself from his own daughter, but in the end I know he's right. I nod and quickly leave the room without looking back.

Guilt fillets my heart as I race down the long, bleak hallway away from my screaming daughter. I don't stop until I can no longer hear her, and I'm safely inside the women's bathroom.

And then I begin to pray.

Please, God, I beg, tears rolling down my face. *Please heal her; don't let her suffer. Give it all to me. Let me take her pain. She's just a child and doesn't understand. I'll suffer for her. She's innocent, not me.*

I can't stand to see my reflection in the mirror, as if somehow this is all my fault. I cry for a long time, praying and begging that everything will be all right. When I've cried the last of my tears, I realize, or hope, that Ashlyn is done. I quickly splash some water on my face and leave the sterile bathroom.

Aaron finds me a few minutes later and gives me a hug. He no longer looks the stone-faced stranger I saw earlier. In fact, he looks sick. His face is pale and his eyes tired. Ashlyn lies in his arms, resting her head on his shoulder. When her eyes meet mine she reaches for me despite the fact that I'd left her. Her eyes are red and swollen, and great tears have stained her puffy cheeks. I vow never to leave her again, no matter how difficult.

Only Ashlyn sleeps that night. Aaron's already been to the hotel's gym twice, and I've read the same chapter of my book three times. No matter how hard we try to distract ourselves from what is to come, we can't do it. At four in the morning, Aaron crawls into bed and wraps his arms around me. "No matter what happens, it's going to be okay. You know that, right?"

I nod. "This is all so weird. It's like we're living someone else's nightmare."

"It will be over soon, and then we'll at least know what we're dealing with. That's half the problem, not knowing."

An hour later, we wake Ashlyn and head to the hospital. She's in surgery for several hours. The waiting room is torture. Its walls bleed sadness, and the heavy air threatens to suffocate me.

After a few hours pass, an elderly woman dressed entirely

in black approaches us. Her white name tag says "Sue: grief counselor." I feel the blood drain from my face and seep into the worn carpet, hardened by the tears of the brokenhearted. My nails dig into my husband's hand, but he lets me.

"Is something wrong?" Aaron asks the woman before she has a chance to speak.

Sue sits down in front of us with a forced smile and eyebrows pulled tightly together. If she doesn't start speaking soon I think I might strangle her. Finally, Sue speaks. "I wanted to see how you two were doing?"

"Fine," I say. "But how's Ashlyn?"

Her stiff eyebrows raise. "Is that who's in surgery?"

I look at Aaron and then back at her. "Yes, but if you don't know that then why are you here?"

"I'm just going around to see if anyone needs to talk. This," she motions her arm around the room, "can be hard on parents."

Aaron leans forward. "Not really, but do you want to know what's hard?"

The woman frowns.

Aaron continues. "When we're waiting for our daughter to come out of risky surgery, and we see a woman who looks like a nun and wearing a name tag that says "grief counselor," and she approaches with an expression the grim reaper would be jealous of!" He leans back, chest heaving.

Sue looks down at her outfit, probably for the first time that day. And then it dawns on her and her eyes widen. "I am so sorry," she stutters. "I'm sure your daughter is just fine." She blubbers on for a few more minutes, but when we hear: "Parents of Ashlyn McClellan?" we stand up.

A smiling nurse says, "Your daughter is in recovery. You can see her now."

I hold myself back from running. When I find Ashlyn, she's lying on her stomach, sleeping. Several tubes are attached to her body.

"The surgeon will come speak with you in a few minutes," a nurse tells us.

We sit down, staring at our sleeping girl who looks more like one of those pod people in the movie *The Matrix*. I stroke her head. "She looks good, considering," I say.

Aaron's on the other side of the bed, holding her hand. He nods.

Ten minutes later, the doctor finds us. "The surgery went well. We got as much of the tumor as we could."

"What does that mean?" I ask.

"We could only get so close to her spinal column so a portion of it had to stay."

"Will she have problems in the future?"

The doctor inhales. "It depends on if the tumor starts growing again. She'll have to come back to the hospital twice a year for the next few years to make sure it's not growing, and then after that you'll need to watch for abnormalities like pain in the legs, difficulty walking, urinary problems. Basically anything out of the ordinary."

"Could you tell if the tumor was malignant?" Aaron asks.

He shakes his head. "Not yet, but we'll know tomorrow."

"What now?" I ask.

The doctor looks down at Ashlyn. "In a few hours we'll move her to a normal room. She'll have to remain on her belly for at least three days."

"Will I be able to hold her?"

He shakes his head. "Unfortunately, no. She needs to remain as still as possible to give her spine a chance to heal."

Thinking exactly what I am, Aaron asks, "So how are we supposed to keep her still?"

"Medication will help, but it will be hard."

Hard was an understatement. As soon as Ashlyn wakes, she wants to be held. She cries for a long time, calling my name, but I never leave her. I caress her head and back, and when I can I lie next to her.

The best news comes when we are told the tumor is benign. The snake-like pressure that had been constricting my heart for the last few months disappears.

On the last day, they let us hold Ashlyn for the first time. It's the best feeling in the world. After a good long cuddle from both her father and mother, we take her for a ride in a child-size wagon.

As we move down the hallway and see other children, I realize how fortunate we are. Our experience could've been so much worse. My gaze meets those of other moms whose children are sick, and an unspoken understanding passes between our small smiles. We know each other's heartache, for we have all experienced that one moment where we have begged God to take the suffering from our child and give it to us.

And we would take the pain, a hundred times over if necessary.

Why?

Because we are the Mommies.

About the Author

Once upon a time, in a wonderful and carefree world, Rachel McClellan fell asleep in a warm and spacious bed, her long hair in great locks around her and not a single blemish upon her face. Outside her window, birds sang and the cloudless blue sky was full of promise.

However, when she awoke, she discovered gum in her now ratted hair, a tiny, chocolate fingerprint smeared across her forehead, and four very wiggly children crowding her bed. There were no birds singing outside her window (or perhaps she couldn't hear them anymore), only a tornado, pulsing with thunder and lightning. Her world was in chaos, a raging storm on all fronts.

But what a perfect storm it was . . .

0 26575 11152 1